"Best thing you ever tasted. Right?"

With a run of his tongue across his lips, he stared at her. "Yeah, and the cookie's not half-bad, either."

"I want to—" Before her brain stopped her, she pressed her lips to his mouth, and her body leaned into him.

Daniel didn't resist. His arm snaked around her waist and tightened his hold, drawing her to him. He took over, parting her lips, exploring her mouth, holding her captive with his caress.

Lord, he could kiss.

Forget chocolate. She had a whole new favorite taste. Raven wrapped her arms around his neck and held him closer, taking the kiss even deeper.

With a groan he eased back. "This is a bad idea," he said softly.

"I don't care," she whispered against his mouth. And she didn't. She just wanted to feel.

THE CRADLE CONSPIRACY

ROBIN PERINI

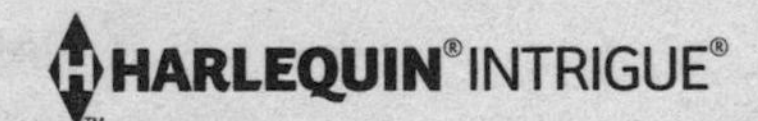

Dedicated to the warriors from all walks of life who battle post-traumatic stress disorder, and the families who fight beside them every minute of every hour of every day. May your journey find light, hope, love and peace.

ISBN-13: 978-0-373-69732-8

THE CRADLE CONSPIRACY

This edition published by arrangement with Harlequin Books S.A.

For questions and comments about the quality of this book, please contact us at CustomerService@Harlequin.com.

Printed in U.S.A.

ABOUT THE AUTHOR

Award-winning author Robin Perini's love of heart-stopping suspense and poignant romance, coupled with her adoration of high-tech weaponry and covert ops, encouraged her secret inner commando to take on the challenge of writing romantic suspense novels. Her mission's motto: "When danger and romance collide, no heart is safe."

Devoted to giving her readers fast-paced, high-stakes adventures with a love story sure to melt their hearts, Robin won a prestigious Romance Writers of America Golden Heart Award in 2011. By day she works for an advanced technology corporation, and in her spare time you might find her giving one of her many nationally acclaimed writing workshops or training in competitive small-bore-rifle silhouette shooting. Robin loves to interact with readers. You can catch her on her website, www.robinperini.com, and on several major social-networking sites, or write to her at P.O. Box 50472, Albuquerque, NM 87181-0472.

Books by Robin Perini

HARLEQUIN INTRIGUE

1340—FINDING HER SON
1362—COWBOY IN THE CROSSFIRE
1381—CHRISTMAS CONSPIRACY
1430—UNDERCOVER TEXAS
1465—THE CRADLE CONSPIRACY

CAST OF CHARACTERS

Raven—With no memory except the sound of a baby's cry, can she trust the dangerous man who found her buried alive—or is he the one who left her for dead?

Daniel Adams—After barely surviving torture in a foreign prison, all he wants is to forget his past and the PTSD he can't shake. Can he overcome his demons in time to save a desperate woman from a mysterious killer?

Hondo Rappaport—A man with his own mysteries, he allowed Daniel and Raven to stay at his motel, no questions asked. Then he threatened them. Whose side is he on?

Sheriff Garrett Galloway—He'll do anything to keep the peace in the town of Trouble, Texas, including look the other way.

Noah Bradford—Able to track anyone anywhere, this deadly spy knows too much about Daniel's past *not* to be dangerous.

Pamela Winter—She's created the perfect family—if only she can protect them.

Christopher Winter—Back from the army, has he learned to bury the memories of abuse?

Elijah Samuels—The newest member of Covert Technology Confidential (CTC), this forensic specialist handles a gun and a test tube with equal precision, but will his results bring more grief than answers?

Chelsea Rivera—All she longed for was to keep her secrets safe and protected. Now she just wants to stay alive.

Chapter One

She came to slowly, her head throbbing, crippling pain skewering her temple like an ice pick digging deep. Without opening her eyes, she tried to lift her hand to touch the side of her head, but her arm wouldn't move, almost as if it were pinned against her body. Confusion swept over her, and she forced her eyes open to sheer, cloying darkness. The air around her was fetid and stale, stinking of dirt, wet wool and…

And blood.

Oh, God. Where was she? Desperation clutched at her throat.

She struggled to move, but her arms were numb. Something held her as if she were encased in a straitjacket. Frantic, she lifted her head, and her face bumped up against what felt like cheap shag carpet. She clawed her fingers beneath her and identified the distinctive weave. This couldn't be happening.

Instinctively she gasped for air, the darkness pressing down like a vise clamped on her chest.

Was she buried alive?

Her stomach rolled, and bile rose in her throat. She couldn't get sick. She had to escape.

She twisted and turned, struggling against the suffocating prison, scratching at the rough fabric. It was above her, below her, around her. She fought to free herself, panic mounting from deep within.

She rocked back and forth. Dirt and dust shook free. She sucked in a breath, and her lungs seized on the foul air. She had to get out.

"Help," she tried to scream, then fell to coughing as if she'd used up the meager air supply.

Worse, the rug had muffled the sound of her voice. Wherever she was buried, would anyone hear her cries? "Oh, God. Someone help me. Please," she croaked in a voice she didn't recognize.

Her breathing turned shallow. The air had thinned.

She sucked in one more desperate breath and froze, aware of a new scent, far more subtle than the rest. It penetrated her mind. Sweet, familiar, and so very, very wrong. Baby lotion.

Nausea suddenly churned, and her dread escalated. Strange visions stirred through her. A pink blanket. A tiny crib. But along with the images came stabbing pain in her head that nearly shattered her.

Her thoughts grew fuzzy, and she fought to hold on to reality. Somehow she knew, if she closed her eyes, she would never wake up. She couldn't pass out. She had to find…

A name flitted at the dark edges of her memory, then slipped away, leaving despair and terror. She turned toward the sweet scent again and breathed deeper. More flashes. Pain. Fear.

A stranger's voice screaming, "No!"

Lights exploded behind her eyelids and darkness engulfed her, closing around one wisp of memory.

The last sound she heard was a baby's terrified cry.

THE AFTERNOON SUN beat down on Daniel Adams from a bright West Texas sky. He adjusted his dusty brown Stetson to block the back of his neck and stood at a fork in the road, not a cloud in sight, not a car to be seen, nothing to tempt him to travel one way more than the other. He could choose a twisting blacktop leading into the Guadalupe Mountains or the county road veering east.

The dirt road headed in the general direction of Carder, Texas. He had friends there who'd made it clear he had a place waiting at Covert Technology Confidential. Staffed with former Special Forces, CIA and FBI operatives, CTC helped people in big trouble with nowhere to turn. The only rule they followed: justice.

Daniel wanted to be there, but he couldn't put himself back into the battle.

Not yet.

He was still too screwed up from his imprisonment and torture in the small European country of Bellevaux. Right now all he wanted was to find his way back to normal from the PTSD and not eat a bullet like his old man had done to deal with the same thing.

Daniel looked around again, frustrated he couldn't even decide which way to go next.

He *normally* made split-second, life-or-death decisions, but that was before. Before he'd been thrown in a dungeon, before the bastards had taken a whip to every inch of his body, an iron bar to his legs, and so flayed his mind with lies and threats that he'd almost broken.

For what seemed like an eternity, he'd fought every damn day with every ounce of strength to stay alive, to not give the interrogator the information he'd wanted.

In the end, Daniel had prayed for death.

Like his old man.

But Daniel was still alive. He'd been found, then stuck full of tubes and even now had more metal holding him together than Wolverine. Against the odds the doctors had given him, he'd healed, then stood and, after six months of recovery in the States, had walked again.

Daniel was broken. He knew it; the CTC operatives knew it. Only his family and his therapist held out hope. *Talk about delusional.* Daniel knew better.

What other reason would a man sleep outside and walk the highways and dirt roads from Langley, Virginia, ending up in Texas months later? A bit Forrest Gump, but Daniel couldn't face his team till he knew his PTSD didn't endanger anyone, until the memories and flashbacks no longer turned him into a terrified beast, striking out at everyone. So here he was, facing miles of desert plateaus, prickly pears and the occasional rattler.

Alone. Mostly.

Trouble followed him. Literally.

Trouble was the name he'd given the foolish dog he'd rescued, who'd warily taken up residence about ten feet from Daniel's side. He glanced at the mixed breed—some odd combination of Newfoundland and Irish setter that made him look like Chewbacca. *Dog must be dying in this heat with all that fur.*

Daniel knelt down and slid the duffel from his shoulder. He tugged a metal bowl from one pocket and set it on the ground. He didn't dwell on why he'd taken to carrying it with him; he just filled the dish half full from his canteen. He rose and stared at the water, then the dog. "What are you waiting for?"

Trouble tilted his head and sat on his haunches, his expression all but saying, *Move back, stupid. You know how this works.*

Daniel sighed and retreated. "Fine. But one of these days, you're going to have to come closer than ten feet."

As soon as Daniel reached the required distance, the

mutt bounded to the water, burying his face in the cool liquid.

Daniel had found the fuzz face lying on the side of the road with his leg and hip scraped up after losing a one-sided battle with a car. Since Trouble wouldn't let Daniel touch him, Daniel had been forced to rig a makeshift travois and drag the miserable canine five miles to a vet's office. The doc tranquilized the dog and patched up his injuries, but the moment the vet had given him the opportunity, Trouble had hightailed it out the front door and down a back alley.

A couple miles later, the animal had taken up residence parallel to Daniel, walking along the highway, never again getting close enough for even a scratch behind the ears. They'd passed a road sign, listing Trouble, Texas, three hundred miles away, and the dog instantly had a name.

That was a couple of weeks ago. The dog limped less now, Daniel a bit more.

Yesterday they'd made it to the small Texas town bearing the dog's name. Daniel had stood in the cramped, dark foyer of a B and B, testing his body's reaction to it, but knew he still couldn't sleep inside. Nothing to do but move on.

The waitress at the diner had told him there was nothing but lost dreams for miles around. She hadn't been lying. The beat-up sign he now leaned against—Cottonwood Creek Copper Mine—could've come from the 1950s.

He really had traveled west of hell to end up a few miles east of nowhere.

Trouble finished his water, nosed the empty bowl toward Daniel, then moved away.

"We're a pair, aren't we, boy?" Daniel said softly. "Too damaged to do anyone any good."

As Daniel repacked the dish, the dog's ears perked up, and he growled low in his throat.

"What's the matter with you?" Daniel turned to see what had upset Trouble and noticed a black vulture circling nearby. "Relax. It's probably eyeing the carcass of a cow that wandered away from the herd."

The dog's hackles rose as he focused his attention on a hill jutting up from the desert. Without a backward glance, Trouble bolted toward the mound. And that vulture.

What the hell? The dog hadn't left Daniel's sight since they'd become traveling companions. "Trouble!" The hairs on the back of Daniel's neck rose, and a warning chill ran through him. He started after the dog that had disappeared from view.

Within a minute the mutt bounded toward Daniel, skidding to a halt a few feet away. Trouble barked urgently several times, ran back a short distance, then turned and barked again.

"What's going on, boy? Show me."

Trouble whined and yipped, then ran. Daniel, his gait uneven, took off after the dog.

The vulture still circled but lower now.

He followed Trouble over the small rise, past a dead rabbit, then came to an abrupt halt.

Trouble circled in front of the dilapidated opening to an old mine, the mouth leading into the dark interior of the mountain. When he saw Daniel, the dog barked again and raced into the tunnel.

A mine shaft. Complete with a condemned sign and evidence of a partial cave-in. Rock walls, claustrophobic darkness. He couldn't go in there. Daniel sucked in a panicked breath, trying to quell his racing heart and the terror that bubbled up from his gut.

The dog didn't come out of the mine.

While Daniel watched, more loose stones fell from the mine's ceiling. "Trouble!"

The dog appeared several feet inside the opening and barked furiously.

Perspiration slid down Daniel's temple. He couldn't do it. Not now. Not ever. The dog growled, racing back and forth, entreating Daniel to follow.

Bracing himself, Daniel stepped barely into the opening, kicking something metal that clanged off the rocks, like the slamming of iron prison bars. A medieval dungeon. Memories assaulted him. The darkness echoing with screams. No, he was in a mine shaft. Still, he heard the footsteps of his captor. The crack of the bastard's whip.

Daniel fell to his knees, fighting to stay present, to escape the horrific memories, until Trouble dropped something in front of Daniel and bit his sleeve. Daniel broke free, panting, and his hand landed on a woman's shoe. Daniel's gut clenched. High heels weren't exactly appropriate for trudging around the Texas desert.

Hell. Was there a woman in here?

Trouble grabbed his shirt again and tugged hard. Daniel snagged a small but powerful flashlight clipped to his belt and shone the beam into the tunnel. The crumbling shaft veered left, debris and broken supports everywhere. Trouble bolted ahead and waited at the bend.

Grasping at his primary PTSD tool, Daniel focused on the grounding techniques he'd learned in therapy and forced himself forward into the shadows. An all-too-familiar panic squeezed his lungs. The walls pressed in until the cave morphed into a stone cell.

Pain level, eight.

Fighting to stay in the present, Daniel clutched the flashlight in a white-knuckled grip. He stared at the illuminated circle, narrowing his gaze. Sounds still reverberated. Trouble's barks morphed into sadistic laughter. The dirt seemed to hold the scent of torture and blood.

He fought against every survival instinct that raged within, that urged him to run. Struggling for control, Daniel moved forward. He wasn't in Bellevaux, he was in Texas. Broken, but free.

"Anyone here?" he shouted.

His words echoed in the darkness, but only silence answered him.

A sprinkling of dirt fell on his head, and the timbers creaked. He froze. The flashlight's beam hit a large heap of rocks, filling half the tunnel.

"Trouble?" Where the hell had the dog gone?

Suddenly he heard an odd moan coming from around the tunnel bend. Was that Trouble…or a human?

"Hello? Is someone there?"

Trouble barked, then reappeared to tug on Daniel's pant leg, frantic now.

Daniel followed the dog into the blackness, concentrating on the small beam of light that helped him keep the nightmares at bay.

The dog rounded the debris and led Daniel to a six-foot-long pile of rocks and dirt, hidden behind the mound from a cave-in. The dog scrabbled among the rocks, desperately trying to dig through them.

Daniel knelt down just as several stones fell away, revealing a bloodstained patch of multicolored carpet and silvery-gray tape.

Duct tape.

Another high-heeled shoe lay a few feet from the mound, and a quiet wail sounded again from beneath the rocks.

Trouble whined and pawed at the carpet.

A steely calm came over Daniel, not complete, but

closer than he'd felt in almost a year. Someone was alive and needed him.

His damn freak-out would have to wait until later. He needed to keep it together now.

After propping the flashlight so he could see, he shoved several rocks to the side. The smell of blood hit him, nearly slamming him into a flashback, but he fought for control.

Daniel swept aside the small rocks that covered the carpet, then threw the larger ones to the side.

"Help me..." The voice faded to silence.

He grabbed the Bowie from his leg sheath and slashed through the two taped areas with the knife, then rolled the carpet open. A woman, beaten and bloody, lay half-comatose on the filthy carpet.

Daniel pressed his fingers against her throat and felt the thread of a pulse.

She was chilled and in rough shape, but alive.

Relief loosened some of Daniel's tenuous hold on his emotions, so he quickly ran his hands over her arms and legs, knowing he needed to get them both out of this death trap fast. His examination didn't reveal any broken bones or severe lacerations on her body, but blood caked one side of her face and hair. The rest of her long hair spread across the carpet like a raven's wings.

He'd seen enough of the birds growing up in Texas, and he'd befriended one in Bellevaux while on surveillance. Sitting in the tree above his hideout, for the price of a few breadcrumbs the damn bird had kept Daniel from going insane while he'd been stuck in one location for weeks. After being forced into that godforsaken dungeon, Daniel had imagined the raven's life. Outside his cell. Outside the prison. Free. Daniel would imagine being free someday like the raven, and used the memory as a lifeline when the world had seemed hopeless.

Maybe this was a sign?

Or maybe he had totally lost his mind, and it was just dawning on him now.

The ground trembled slightly.

Daniel cursed, then scooped her into his arms and stood. "Let's go, Trouble."

The woman's eyes opened, gorgeous, fear-filled eyes, the color of cinnamon. "Who are you? Did I come here with you?"

"I'm not the one who put you here," he said. A rumble sounded from somewhere overhead. He let out a curse. "We're in an unstable mine, and we have to get out. Now."

Her eyes widened. He clutched her close against his chest and took off toward the bend.

The mountain shook again, then a spray of dirt and debris showered over both of them before one of the ceiling supports gave way with a loud crack.

"Cave-in!" Daniel curled her beneath him and covered her with his body, hoping she wasn't bleeding internally. And hoping to hell the roaring panic slamming through his mind didn't make him explode. They were being buried alive, and he was losing it fast.

DIRT AND ROCKS pelted the ground around her, but they didn't hit or hurt her. The man lying on top of her let out a soft grunt, his broad shoulders protecting her from the onslaught.

The dog she'd seen momentarily, before all hell broke loose in the cave, now sidled up against her and whined, burying his cold nose against her hand. She grabbed its fur, then slowly released her grip enough to pet it, trying to calm the animal's fears as well as her own.

The man groaned and shifted against her; the contours of his hips and thighs settled over her, pinning her down.

She took a panicked breath. Who was he? She couldn't remember him, and yet he'd protected her.

And why had he said he wasn't the one who put her here?

She couldn't be sure of anything with the incessant pounding in her head. Her mind spun with confusion. A bevy of rocks cascaded down the wall, thudding on the ground. At any moment the cave could bury them both.

She knew they had to escape but couldn't focus on anything except the feel of strong arms holding her and the hard body shielding her from the cave-in. She couldn't let reality in because something was horribly, horribly wrong. She was supposed to be somewhere. Doing…something. Something important but she couldn't remember what.

Her heart seized, and she struggled to regain control.

"Hey, you okay?" the man on top of her whispered. "I'm going to try to move and see what shape we're in."

As he spoke, his warm breath caressed her ear, helping her relax a bit. She didn't know why, but she felt safe with him. Which was stupid, considering where they were.

The mountain around them rumbled again, and she trembled, gripping his shirt. He wrapped her closer, pressing her cheek against his chest. Despite his calm demeanor, his heart raced. Did he think they would die here? Her head throbbed like the devil pummeling his way into heaven, but she didn't want to move. She didn't want to know they were trapped.

When the tremors stopped, he raised his head. She blinked and stared at his face. The beam from the flashlight had gone dim in the dust, but she could make out his features. Barely. His dirt-filled hair fell over his forehead and nearly reached his chin. The scar down one side of his cheek made him look like a pirate, and the hard pulsing line of his jaw seemed to confirm her worst fears. "Are we going to die?"

The shadow that swept through his hazel eyes was there and gone so fast she thought she'd imagined it.

"No."

"Thank you, if you're lying." She reached up to his face and touched his cheek, his jaw still clenched, contradicting his assurances.

He met her gaze, and his eyes flashed with gold. "Are you hurt?"

She tried to sit up, but rocks surrounded them. Oh, dear God, how would they get out of here? She couldn't breathe. Her head throbbed worse whenever she moved, and her heart thudded against her chest like she had run a sprint. The feeling that she had to do something struck again. What was she supposed to be doing? Every time she tried to focus, pain stabbed through her brain, triggering flashes of light and odd sounds…and terror.

"My head feels like it's going to explode, and I'm seeing double. I can't think."

She struggled to rise, and the world grayed. She clutched at his shirt, twisting the fabric hard. She panted and stared at him, unblinking, willing the world to come into focus.

The first thing she noticed was the bloodstained carpet, and she gasped. "Was I inside that?"

The man backed away, preparing to stand aside, but she clung to his cotton shirt. She didn't want him to leave. She needed him close. He was the only thing real in this craziness. "Someone tried to kill me, didn't they?" she asked, pressing her hand to her bloodied forehead.

She should know the answer, but her entire mind was blank.

"I don't know what happened," he whispered, his voice deepening. He stroked the back of her hand, his touch gentle but steady. “But you’re fine. Just breathe in. I need you calm for us to escape.”

His gaze held her captive. He took in a deep but shaky breath.

She did the same. The dog pushed against her leg, and she curled her fingers in its fur again. Daniel exhaled, and she mimicked him, breath for breath. Unable to look away, she pinned her focus on him, inhaling through her nose, letting her lungs expand and fill.

Her grip eased a bit on his shirt, but not enough that she couldn’t feel the rapid heartbeat beneath her hand. “Are *you* okay?”

Something dark and haunted crossed his face again. A second later it was gone.

“I’m fine, but you’ve got a hell of a knot on your head.”

She raised her hand and felt the swelling and the sticky residue. A small whine escaped her. “It hurts.”

“I bet it does.” He pressed his fingers gently against her scalp. “Why don’t you sit back down and drink while I dig us out.” He tugged a canteen from his belt, tilting it against her lips.

Gratefully she let the water sluice down her throat. “Thank you.” Her voice cleared somewhat.

She took another sip. “How did you find me?”

“Trouble must have heard you.” The man turned and started pulling stones to the side to clear the passageway.

“Trouble?”

“The dog. I’m Daniel, by the way.” He threw a large rock farther away. “And your name?”

She opened her mouth, and nothing came out. Why couldn’t she think of it? Everyone knew their own name. In an instant the crushing pain was back. The flashes of light. Muffled cries and hazy images. Trying desperately to stop her head from spinning, she clutched the heart-shaped locket around her neck like a good-luck talisman. "Oh, my God…"

Daniel turned around at the panic in her voice.

"I don't know my name." Her hands clutched at his. "Daniel, how can I not know my own name?"

Chapter Two

The dust from the mine filtered the beam from the flashlight, but it was more than enough to let Daniel know they were screwed. Sweat that had nothing to do with exertion slid down his back. He was fighting off a PTSD meltdown and now this. How could he comfort her when he felt borderline psychotic?

He had to get outside. Fast.

"What's my name?" the woman repeated, her voice shaking.

Daniel's grip tightened on the rock he held. He hated the fear and bewilderment in her words, and he'd be damned if he let her see his alarm for both of them.

The blood on her temple oozed again, droplets landing on her dusty silk shirt. Someone had wanted her dead. That person might still succeed if Daniel didn't dig them out quickly. He had no answers for this terrified woman, and couldn't give her much in the way of comfort except to wrap her in his arms and hope she mistook his trembling as her own.

Daniel stroked her dark hair. "You're going to be okay," he reassured, knowing his words may not be true. "Once that bump goes down, you'll remember everything."

"What if I don't?" She shivered.

He pressed her closer. "You will. It's common with head injuries to be a little fuzzy."

She shook her head, then winced, pressing her hand to her temple. "This isn't fuzzy. *I. Can't. Remember. My. Name.*" She paused, her eyes widening, then she whispered, "I can't remember…anything."

Swearing internally, Daniel gently stroked her black hair and forced what he hoped was a confident smile to his face. "Maybe we should call you Trouble. You deserve the moniker more than the mutt over there."

At the sound of his name, Trouble's head cocked.

"Or we could go the princess route. Sleeping Beauty might be appropriate." Daniel kept his tone light, trying to divert her focus…and his. "Except she had blond hair. You could be Snow White. Her hair was black."

A small smile tilted the corners of the woman's mouth. "You're an idiot, but thanks." She bit her lip. "Seriously I can't just pick a name out of thin air."

"Then I'll do it for you." He studied her amazing brown eyes and once more touched the long, silky strands of hair. Black as night. Or *like a raven's wing...* "How about I call you Raven for now? After your hair color. Just until you remember."

"Raven, huh?" she said, her voice small and vulnerable.

"Raven suits you," Daniel admitted. "It's striking and unforgettable. Like you." He pulled back his hand. "Now I have to get back to work."

Methodically he picked up one rock after another, telling himself he'd break through soon. But he could feel the churning in his mind and gut. He took a cleansing breath, praying for control.

His hands grew slippery with sweat. He would not give in to the panic.

The shrinks had diagnosed him with post-traumatic stress disorder soon after his rescue from Bellevaux.

Like Daniel hadn't recognized the symptoms already.

His combat-vet father had suffered from PTSD nightmares and flashbacks as long as Daniel could remember—until his dad had ended it with a bullet to his brain. Daniel had found him, and the sight haunted him still.

At the memory Daniel's heart raced, pounding against his ribs as if it would burst through any second. He closed his eyes to stall another attack.

A furry nose nuzzled its way beneath his hand. What the hell? Now the dog decided to make friends? Daniel's fingers curled through Trouble's coat. If Trouble could work through his issues, Daniel wasn't about to succumb to his. He had no time to wallow in imaginary fears. Even if they felt completely real.

"We'll be fine," he announced, perhaps as much to hear the words aloud as to calm Raven. But he'd noticed it getting harder to breathe with all the dust. He came upon a few large stones, and he lugged them away, one at a time.

Each time he rose to his feet, steadying himself on the leg his captors had broken in three places, it became harder. If his leg gave out, they'd be in a world of hurt. He dragged a wooden beam toward the back and bumped into something. He turned, noticing a big painted box with a large letter *C* carved into the top. One corner of the lid was bloody, with a few pieces of black hair stuck to the surface. It didn't take Sherlock Holmes to recognize the match to Raven's head wound. Besides, kids' toy boxes didn't wind up in deserted mines by accident.

Using the edge of his shirt, Daniel opened the lid. Empty. "Raven? Do you recognize this box?"

Before she could respond, Trouble snapped to attention. He whined and let out a loud bark, pacing back and forth in the confined space. Another rumble sounded from somewhere inside the mountain.

"We're out of time. I think if I pull out a few more rocks, you can get through."

She tried to walk, but her legs buckled beneath her.

He grabbed her, and she held her body stiff. "Forget me. Dig." She pushed on his chest. "Go!"

Another rumble resonated through the earth surrounding them. The mine was collapsing. They had to get out.

Daniel yanked a rock out, then another, speed counting more than finesse now. Within minutes a small hole had appeared.

He shone the light through the opening. The entire cavern beyond was intact. For now.

Raven's small hand clutched his arm as she crawled up beside him. "I can help."

"Raven…"

With two hands she grabbed a rock and tossed it into the pile he'd started. "Shut up and dig."

"Stubborn woman," he grumbled, but he admired her grit.

They worked side by side, and before long, they'd created an opening large enough for her and Trouble to escape. He peered through the hole. "Can you slide through?"

She studied the gap. "I think so. What about you?"

"I'll be fine. Trouble," Daniel ordered, "go on."

The dog looked at Daniel; then the stupid mutt seemed to roll his eyes. He lifted his paws to the hole and climbed through.

Daniel grasped her waist. "Go on. I'll be right behind you."

"Your shoulders won't fit through that opening."

"I'll move a few more rocks, then follow you."

She hesitated. "Promise?"

"Believe me, honey, I want out of here worse than you do."

Finally she nodded and reached her arms into the hole. Trouble whined from the other side. Her body slithered through. The rocks groaned in protest and shuddered around her.

Raven stilled.

Dust and gravel landed on her back.

"Don't stop! Move!" Daniel batted a falling rock away.

Daniel shoved her hips forward, and she tumbled to the ground with a moan, clutching her head. Trouble nudged her cheek, giving her a quick lick.

"Hey! Are you all right?" Daniel asked, as loud as he dared given the avalanche just waiting to happen.

"Yes."

She rose unsteadily and faced him, too wobbly for his liking. He peered at her through the frame of rocks. "Get outside. Stay at least twenty feet from the mine's entrance."

The obstinate woman just shook her head and came toward him. "I won't leave you. I can dig from this side."

Another warning grumbled around them.

"Look, lady. This place is coming down soon. A few more rocks, and I'm running like hell out of here. I don't need to be concerned about you, too."

She hesitated.

Daniel tossed a stone aside. "Don't worry. It takes more than a cave-in to do me in. This little challenge doesn't even break my top five. Now get the hell outside."

With one last look, she stumbled around the bend toward the mine opening.

"Go," Daniel said to Trouble. "Guard her."

A soft whine escaped the dog, but he followed her.

Daniel widened the hole, his adrenaline ratcheting higher with every second. The stubborn woman didn't weigh more than a hundred twenty pounds, and she'd nearly brought the unstable wall down on them. At over two hundred, he might get one shot to reach the other side, but these stones were like the last blocks in Jenga. Very precarious…and dangerous.

If he was going to die, he wanted it to be out in the open, under the sky, not like a rat trapped in a hole. At least the fight to stay alive was beating back the past—just barely.

He tried to squeeze through, but his hulking six-foot-four frame scraped the edges of the passageway. Damn football shoulders.

Two more rocks should do it.

He moved one, and a spray of dirt sifted over him.

One more to go.

Daniel took a deep breath then tugged out the rock and heard the cracking start.

He shoved through the hole, ignoring the rocks hitting his body. He dragged his bad leg through just as the roar grew louder.

Then the whole damn mountain started coming down on top of him.

"DANIEL!" THE GROUND around Raven shook, tossing her to her knees as debris scattered over her.

She'd made it to within three feet of leaving the tunnel, and despite several attempts, she couldn't stagger to her feet. Her aching head spun in the dimming light from outside.

Oh, God, she couldn't leave Daniel alone. He'd rescued her. She had to get up and help him somehow.

Suddenly he burst around the corner, plowed into her and knocked her flat.

"You're supposed to be outside!" He scooped her into

his arms as if she weighed nothing and hauled her outside through a cloud of dust.

Daniel stumbled, and they went down hard, just a few feet outside the cave's opening. Dirt and dust spewed from the mine, raining down on them, but Raven didn't care. They'd made it.

Trouble bounded next to them, barking until Daniel finally rolled onto his back, his face screwed up in agony. He sucked in several gulps of air, then glared at Raven. "What were you thinking? I told you to get out."

"I wanted to help—"

"Are you always this obstinate?" he growled, shifting his leg, his jaw tightening.

"I don't know," she whispered. "I really don't." The blankness in her mind scared her, terrified her. She rubbed her temple. Why did everything seem like a foggy void, one she couldn't see past?

His lips thinned into a grimace, then he sighed. "It's a miracle we made it out in one piece." He scanned up and down her body. "You look like hell. I don't suppose I look much better."

She gazed at his dirt-covered figure. He looked great, actually. His dusty clothes didn't take away from the fact that he appeared every inch the hero. From the stubble on his chin to the mussed light brown hair kissed with sunlight, to the V-shaped body, there wasn't anything to complain about. When he walked over and grabbed a brown Stetson from the ground, dusted it off and settled it on his head, the look was complete.

She didn't know what kind of guy had attracted her before, but this one was doing it for her now. She struggled to a seated position. Actually she was seeing two of him now, which couldn't be a good sign.

"Let me help you up." Daniel held out his hand to her.

"We're in the middle of nowhere, my canteen is behind a wall of rock, and you need a doctor. We have to get moving."

She placed her small hand in his and stood beside him. "I can make it."

He glanced over at her. "I have no doubt of that, honey. We just have to walk to my phone and call the sheriff who patrols these parts. I'd like to try to get you into the shade."

She took a step and swayed into him, then bent over, resting her hands on her knees. Her stomach roiled, and she swallowed down the nausea.

He snuck his arm around her waist. "We'll go slow," he said softly. "It's been a tough day."

She leaned against him but tried to mostly stand on her own two feet. Daniel hadn't said anything, but the hitch in his step told her that he'd been injured. Maybe it was because he'd come to her rescue, but the closer she looked at the scar on his face, she could tell his skin was still healing from recent wounds. He looked like he'd had a rough year, not just a rough day. War veteran, maybe?

The bright sun in the clear blue sky blinded her after the dark mine, so she stared at her feet and concentrated on putting one foot in front of the other. That's all she had to do.

One step.

The world spun a little.

Another step…gray clouded her vision. The darkness enveloped her, blocking out the sun.

From far, far away she heard a loud curse and watched the ground tilt toward her.

Then all went silent.

THE BLAZING SUN hung low in the sky. Daniel's leg protested with every step, his body apparently not thrilled with carrying Raven's extra weight, no matter how slight. Shards of pain dug through the spots where the plate and screws held his bones together. All he could do was keep walking.

He'd tried dialing 9-1-1 for help, but signals in the middle of nowhere were hard to come by. Once he thought someone answered, but he never could connect. Hell, he couldn't even reach Information to get the local sheriff's department number.

Trouble had taken up his customary position out of reach, though instead of ten feet away, the mutt had moved closer. More like six feet, eyeing the woman in Daniel's arms the whole time.

"If you were a horse this would be a lot easier," Daniel groused to his traveling companion.

The dog just quirked his ear and kept walking.

With a quick shift of his arms, Daniel adjusted his burden. Raven had scared him when she'd keeled over. She hadn't responded when he'd attempted to revive her. Head injuries were nothing to mess with, and for a moment, he'd feared the worst.

When her chest had risen and fallen, his heart had restarted. At least she was breathing, even if her face had taken on the color of buttermilk.

He'd debated whether to turn back to Trouble, Texas, or go forward to Nickel Creek, just south of the Texas–New Mexico border. But he knew Trouble had a medical clinic, so for the first time since leaving Langley, Daniel retraced his steps. He still had a good ten miles to go. Even one more seemed impossible right now.

His foot snagged a rock, and he stumbled forward. Daniel's arms held Raven snug against his body, but a sharp pang pierced his knee. Something had stabbed or bitten him. He hadn't heard a rattler. He backed up and righted himself, a long, slow breath escaping him at the sight of the devilishly sharp plant at his feet. The lechuguilla resembled the base of a yucca, but its three-inch-long black spikes at the ends of the flat leaves could spear through leather or skin with ease. Thank God, he'd been moving slow. Those suckers could do some real damage.

He was lucky he hadn't dropped Raven.

The jostling hadn't caused a gasp or the slightest movement from her, and he didn't like it. She'd been out too long. He glanced behind him. As dusk approached, the merciless sunlight dimmed somewhat. Even when he'd been in top shape, it would've taken him until full dark to reach Trouble. His leg wouldn't hold out much longer.

A siren sliced the silence. Daniel tamped down the irrational urge to run in the opposite direction. He had to remind himself he wasn't in a country where the national police could stuff you into a dungeon, and people forgot about you like you were never born.

He waited as the sheriff's vehicle pulled a few feet from him.

A cop stepped out and rounded the car. Not your average small-town sheriff. This guy walked with precision and a determined quiet. He had the look of some of CTC's operatives, and his narrowed expression took in the three of them. "You the one who tried calling 9-1-1? We caught the tower location, and this is one of the only paved roads around. You need some help? Your lady's not looking too good."

"She needs a hospital," Daniel said, shifting her in his arms so the sheriff could see her head wound. "And I need to talk to you."

The man took one look at the blood on her head and ran to his car. He opened the back door and helped Daniel slide inside the idling vehicle with Raven still cradled against him. The dog hesitated by the side door.

"Come on, boy." Daniel tapped the backseat.

The dog hunkered back, then scampered into the desert.

"Trouble!" Daniel called.

The mutt didn't stop, just disappeared behind a shrub bush.

Daniel sighed and gazed at Raven. The cop shut the door on them. "You want me to go after him?"

With a pang, Daniel scanned the empty landscape. Yeah, Daniel wanted the sheriff to go after the dog. Trouble had no water, no food, and it would be dark soon, but Raven was still unconscious. "She needs an emergency room. The dog lands on his feet." At least Daniel prayed Trouble would.

"He yours? Will he go home?"

"I'm not sure either of us currently has a home," Daniel said. "We met on the road."

"I see." The cop pulled onto the road and studied Daniel through the rearview mirror. "You wouldn't be that drifter Milly mentioned who came through town yesterday?"

Daniel stiffened. He didn't like the fact that someone had noticed him. He prided himself on being invisible to most, but the waitress had been way too friendly in that small-town-nosy kind of way.

"She didn't mention you had a traveling companion. You gonna tell me what happened, and why you're carrying an unconscious woman down a county road? Or did you find her along the way, too?"

At the suspicious tone in the sheriff's voice, the hairs on the back of Daniel's neck straightened. He didn't need any more problems, so he told the man what he knew.

The sheriff cursed. "Those mines have been abandoned for years. I occasionally find some kids out there playing stupid games of truth or dare. One kid died because he couldn't find his way out. The state should seal them up."

"You need to get the carpet and the toy box out of there first. Maybe you'll find some fingerprints."

The sheriff plucked his radio speaker. "I don't have a lot of help, but I can call in some assistance from Midland. If it's not too dangerous to enter the mine, they'll retrieve the evidence." He waited a beat. "You say this woman doesn't know her name? Do you believe her?"

Daniel met the sheriff's gaze. He understood what the man was asking. "Wrapped in carpet held together with duct tape? She didn't do that to herself. Yeah, I believe her."

The sheriff zipped across the desert and soon reached the Trouble, Texas, Medical Clinic. Daniel carried Raven inside.

A grizzled doctor took one look at her wounds, grabbed a gurney, then wheeled her into a closed area. Daniel followed.

"You with her?" the nurse asked, obviously ready to evict him.

Daniel nodded. He wasn't about to let Raven out of his sight. Not while she was so vulnerable.

The doctor immobilized her neck first, then bent down. "Can you hear me, miss?" he asked loudly.

She didn't respond at first, until a child in a different examining room cried.

Raven's eyes blinked open, and she stared up at the doctor in panic.

"Where am I? Where's my baby?"

PAMELA WINTER EASED the rocking chair back and forth, back and forth, her aging muscles aching as she held the child closer.

Squeak. Squeak. Squeak. "Mommy's going to take care of you."

The baby cooed in her sleep, pursing those sweet little

lips as if she were nursing. Pamela wished she could do it, but it was impossible at her age.

"You'll be fine, my precious girl."

Pamela let her wrinkled hand stroke down the soft cheeks of the healthy eighteen-month-old baby. So healthy when…

No. Pamela wouldn't think that way. Everything would be fine. She'd done what she had to do.

The television filtered through the room. Another game show, one she'd watched nightly for twenty-five years. The recliner near the fireplace mocked her with its emptiness.

This wasn't the home it was supposed to be. She wasn't supposed to be alone. She was supposed to be here with her husband, with their new daughter. A perfect, happy family. A second chance. A do-over after the horrific way their first attempt at parenthood had turned out. She'd believed her husband had changed. He'd certainly been quieter toward the end. He hadn't used his fists or his threats as much after Christopher left.

Until earlier that day before her husband died.

Pamela hummed a lullaby and touched the rosy cheek of the beautiful baby in her arms. A perfect daughter. Unlike Christopher, the child from hell. A child with no conscience who, even when he grew up, never felt the need for one.

Thank God his father had finally found an alternative. After yet another stupid stunt, he'd told Christopher to choose the army or jail. Christopher had picked the army, so now he was trained to kill, with no conscience to stop him. Pamela shivered, even though the temperature hadn't turned cold. Every day she prayed she'd get a telegram, or a knock at the door, along with a military chaplain saying her son was dead, and the world was a safer place for it.

What a blessing that would be.

A key sounded in the lock. She tensed. Her husband was dead. Her son was gone.

No one should have a key.

"I'm home."

Oh, my God. Christopher.

Pamela vaulted out of her chair, clutching the infant in her arms. What was *he* doing here? Her son wasn't due for leave from deployment for another six months.

She couldn't deal with his horrible temper, his manic and depressive rages. Not now. What was she going to do? He'd kill her if he found out the truth about what she'd done. She settled the baby in the nearby cradle and rose from the rocker.

He could *never* find out.

Heavy steps clunked across the hardwood floor. She bit her lip.

The tall, strapping man, as handsome and dangerous as his father, strode across the room, the once long, shaggy hair now cut military short. He dropped his duffel in the marble-covered foyer.

"No hug for your baby boy?"

He gave her a smile. A smile she hadn't seen since he'd become a teenager.

She allowed herself a smidgen of hope. Was the good Christopher back? She embraced him carefully like one would a cobra. He could be that lethal.

Her son stared at her. "Is the baby sleeping?"

She nodded, her throat closed off in fear. Would he be able to tell?

With a grin, he crossed to the cradle and stared at the infant. "She's even more beautiful than her pictures. Chubby, rosy cheeks. You've been plumping her up. I'm glad. She was so pale in the last set of photos." He kissed the top of the baby's head. "I'm home now, kiddo. Anyone messes with you, and they're dead."

Pamela turned so he wouldn't see the tears trailing down her cheeks, tears that were an all-too-common occurrence these days. Her arms felt empty again. She picked up the baby and then faced her son. Forcing a false smile into place, she reached a trembling hand to Christopher. "I'm glad you're home," she lied. "Safe with us. Safe and sound."

"I opted out early. I'm back for good."

She tried to swallow down the terror that clutched at her heart. This wouldn't work. She couldn't keep the truth from him forever. Someone would tell him, or he would guess.

Why was this happening?

Pamela hadn't thought he could leave the service before his five-year enlistment was up. Nothing had worked out like she'd planned.

Everything was so hard now. So wrong.

The baby squirmed in Pamela's arms and opened her striking green eyes.

"Hello, beautiful," he said, scooping up the baby from his mother's arms.

He walked across the room, past the darkened hearth, then sat in his father's chair, an obvious act of defiance to the man he'd hated.

Christopher examined the infant in his arms. "She reminds me of someone. Who do you think?"

Pamela swallowed, unwilling to answer. She had to get him out of here, away from the baby. She would have to come up with some way to hide the truth.

The television volume rose as a news banner flashed across the screen.

Breaking news. Trouble, Texas.

The picture of a battered and bloody woman took up the entire screen.

Pamela almost cried out in shock at the sight. With a trembling hand, she grabbed the remote and pressed the volume control so she could hear.

"The sheriff's office revealed the woman was found in an abandoned mine west of Trouble. Referred to as Jane Doe, she cannot identify herself due to a head injury. They're asking anyone who knows or has seen this woman to contact them immediately."

Pamela dropped the remote. She glanced at her son, then swayed. "This can't be happening. That woman is supposed to be dead. She tried to steal my baby."

Chapter Three

"Open your eyes, darlin'. Please."

Daniel's soft, deep voice soothed Raven's senses. She wanted to do what he asked, but she couldn't seem to function. She hurt too much. The rhythmic pulses slammed in her temples like a bass drum reverberating through her mind. She wanted to let sleep overtake her again, except for some urgent feeling that drove her to wake up and move. She needed help for some reason. *His help.* For something very important…

Dazed, she struggled to lift her lids. Through her lashes, unfamiliar images coalesced. The room was dark, save a low light glowing from above the headboard. An IV and monitor were hooked up by her bed. Panic started, then she heard someone speak again.

"That's it. Wake up now. Just a little more."

It *was* Daniel. What a relief. She knew his voice. Trusted his voice.

A callused finger traced her forehead, and she peered blearily over at the fuzzy double image of the man sitting beside her.

"There you go. Keep those beautiful eyes open."

"Daniel." His face, handsome and troubled, held her enthralled. He was familiar. The only thing that was. She reached up and touched his cheek, the one with the scar.

He clasped her hand in his and drew it away. “Don’t exert yourself. Are you really awake this time?” he asked. “Awake enough to answer some questions?”

“I think so,” she croaked.

Daniel gave her a small smile, and she could see the relief in his eyes.

“But I don’t know where I am.”

“We’re in Trouble, Texas, at their medical clinic. You had me worried, passing out like you did.”

She licked her lips. Her mouth was so dry. “My head hurts. I can’t think straight.”

“I’ll tell the nurse. Want some water?” he asked.

“Please.”

He cupped her head and held a straw next to her lips. With one sip, the cold fluid coated her throat. She smiled at him. He knew just what she needed.

Even that small movement made the throbbing restart. She lifted her hand to her temple and encountered a bandage. “What’s this? What happened?”

“Before or after the cave-in?” he asked.

“Cave-in?” Hazy images of darkness and falling rocks assailed her. The scent of panic and fear, from a…a dog and Daniel. Dust. Blood. There were some memories there, but none were very clear. She touched the bandage once more. “How did I do this? Did the rocks hit me? What was I doing in a stupid cave anyway?”

“I don’t know the answers to all your questions, but falling rocks only did some of the damage.” He leaned forward, glancing at the curtain. “Look, I don’t have much time before someone comes in, but I do want to help you. Can you try to think about being in the mine shaft before it caved in? Do you remember who hurt you?”

“Someone hurt me?” She furrowed her brow, trying to

reconstruct the strange images in her mind. "Why would anyone do that?"

"Think. What do you remember?" he asked.

"My name is Raven."

"Raven's not your name." The man's expression held nothing but pity. "We made it up because you were panicked about not remembering yours."

"That's crazy." She dug her fingernails into his palm. "That's the only name I know. And I know you. You were holding me and telling me everything would be all right. We were in the cave together. You held me. I remember you."

He squeezed her hand. "I was only holding you to calm you down. I'm sorry. We never met before today."

"It doesn't seem possible. You're...you're Daniel. I know you." She grasped at the small straw of sanity remaining. "I was in your arms. How can you deny we know each other? Why are you lying?"

The curtain surrounding them was yanked back, the sound of the metal rings scraping like nails on a chalkboard.

A man in uniform entered the room. "Yeah, Adams, that's something I'd like to know. You sure looked involved with her when I saw you."

"I was trying to save her life. What was I supposed to do? Dump her and run?"

"No, but you informed the charge nurse you were together when you arrived. You were in the exam room the whole time. Didn't look like a total stranger situation to me. So what gives?"

A deep-seated fear took hold in Raven's chest when anger rose to Daniel's face.

He slowly stood and faced the lawman. "My dog found her, and I tried to get her help. End of story."

"I also warned you not to come back here alone with the Jane Doe. You make a habit of going against the law? You got a prison record somewhere I should check out?"

Daniel blanched, darkness in his eyes once more. "You go ahead and check."

"I intend to," the sheriff shot back. "Now, why don't you wait outside, while I have a talk with this lady you claim not to know."

Raven gripped Daniel's hand. He was her only touchstone. "Please, don't make him leave."

"I'm Sheriff Galloway, ma'am." His gaze sliced across Daniel. "It appears you've been the victim of a crime. I need to ascertain the threat. I said, step away from her, Mr. Adams."

Daniel glanced at their intertwined fingers. "Why don't you let the lady decide, Sheriff? She doesn't look all that eager to be alone with you."

"I said move away." Galloway grabbed Daniel by the arm. "Don't press me. You're two seconds from a cell."

Daniel yanked his arm from Galloway's grasp and pushed aside the curtain.

"Don't leave, Adams. I'm talking to you next."

Not attempting to cloak his obvious fury, Daniel settled against the wall just outside the partition.

Raven couldn't believe what was happening. None of this made sense.

"That man claims he doesn't know you, ma'am," the sheriff said, pulling a small notebook from his uniform pocket. "Yet you say you *do* know him. Which is it?"

Her gaze went back and forth between the two men. "I…I don't know."

"Did Adams hurt you?"

Did he? She was already injured when she came to in the mine. She pressed her hand against her head. That damned throbbing was getting worse, scrambling her thoughts. "I…I don't think so." She blinked hard against the blur Daniel's face had become. "I think he just helped me. I can't really remember what happened before the cave-in."

"So he could have put you there?"

"No. He specifically told me he didn't do that."

"What?" Galloway strode out to Daniel. "Okay, Adams, that's it. You're coming with me until I sort this out." The sheriff slapped a cuff on Daniel's wrist.

Daniel stilled, his face stiff as he stared at the silver bracelet. "Great, just great. Good Samaritan bites the dust one more time. When will I learn?"

Raven stared at him in handcuffs, horrified. Her mind whirled in confusion. She didn't think he had hurt her, but could she be wrong? Nothing made sense.

His gaze went flat, the light behind his eyes dimming. Expressionless, lifeless, soulless. Instinctively Raven reached out to him, needing something, anything to hold on to, but Daniel turned away from her. "I guess I know where I'm headed. Thanks, sweetheart."

The sheriff snagged his prisoner's free arm and snapped the second cuff closed, pinning his arms behind him. The loud click echoed in the room, and Daniel's jaw throbbed, his neck muscles bunched together. He didn't look back at her.

She wanted to call out to Daniel, but she didn't know what to say. She just couldn't remember. She had to be Raven. Didn't she?

Then why had he lied about not knowing her?

"I…don't…remember." The words stuttered from her. Desperation clawed at her insides.

The sheriff gave her a sympathetic grimace. "If Adams

is telling the truth, he'll be out soon. If not…you have nothing to be sorry about. You're safe now."

Sheriff Galloway escorted Daniel out.

The nurse whipped the curtain closed, shutting her in. Alone. Abandoned. The cream-covered cloth fluttered still, a barrier to the world. She wrapped her arms around her body, trying to stop the aching loneliness. Her hands and heart felt empty.

She turned to her side in the bed, staring at the curtained wall. She didn't blink. Her vision grew blurry. Why couldn't she remember? Try as she might, just a few glimmers sifted through her. A fuzzy dog's face, a toy box, *and Daniel.*

She sighed. Daniel. What had she done? Why hadn't she defended him? Why hadn't she fought to make the sheriff understand that she felt safe with Daniel? She reached out her hand, wishing his strong fingers were there for her to grasp.

Her belly clenched. She had the unsettling feeling she'd just made a terrible mistake in letting Daniel go. She curled into a ball. Her fingernails bit into her palm.

Oh, God, what had she done?

THE NIGHTMARE WOULDN'T end. Raven knew she was asleep, but she couldn't escape. Wrapped in a carpet. The dust, the dirt, the blood.

She fought against the memory suffocating her, struggling to break free from the prison. Her hands clenched at her side. Not carpet. Sheets.

The clinic. And a presence watching over her. She could feel its malevolence.

She squeezed her eyes tighter, unable to battle the unexpected terror seizing her body and her mind. She swallowed and forced herself to open her eyes.

"Daniel?" she mumbled, praying he was there, despite her letting him down.

Her blurry vision focused. A man stood above her, his face half-hidden by a surgical mask. Not Daniel though and not the doctor who'd treated her before.

"Who—"

Before she could ask, he pressed his fingers around her throat, then clamped his other hand over her mouth and nose. He tightened his grip, cutting off all air.

Please, God. She couldn't breathe. She twisted against him, each movement sending shafts of pain and light through her brain. He pressed harder, then braced himself and used his knee to hold her to the bed. He was crushing her windpipe.

Panicked, she grappled for the call button, but he yanked it from her hand. White spots filled her graying vision. She couldn't die this way. She wouldn't.

Frantic, relying on pure instinct, Raven used all of her remaining strength to drive the flat of her palm into the man's nose as hard as she could. She heard the crunch of breaking bone.

Her attacker yelled and stumbled back, blood spewing over his mask.

A string of expletives exploded, and he slammed his fist into her head. Pain like a thousand pieces of shrapnel penetrating her skull shattered her control, but she had one chance to live.

Screaming for help, she clutched her head and curled up to protect herself.

Shouting and approaching footsteps sounded from beyond the curtain.

"Damn it!" Her assailant, wearing a white doctor's coat over jeans, shoved through the curtain, covered with his own blood. He slammed a metal cart to the side and barreled over the doctor.

Raven struggled to take in air through her damaged throat. She heard frantic cries to call the sheriff, and the thud and crash of more bodies and equipment hitting the floor.

The doctor staggered to her side, blood streaming down the side of his face. “Are you all right? What happened?”

“That man tried to kill me,” Raven croaked. “I need Daniel. Someone please get me Daniel.”

The doctor yelled out some orders then bent over her. “Stay with me, Raven. Don’t give up.”

She blinked through the agonizing pain. All she wanted to do was sleep. She couldn’t keep her eyes open. She sucked in a shallow breath. She should have trusted her gut. She should have trusted Daniel.

She *had* made a horrible mistake. She just prayed Daniel wouldn’t hold it against her.

THE JAIL CELL was too small.

Daniel lay rigid on the bunk and stared at the tiles on the ceiling, counting the dotted patterns within them. He refused to look at the gray cinder-block walls, and he sure as hell wouldn’t look at the bars holding him in this prison.

Cringing and screaming on the floor, fighting off phantoms only he could see, would go a long way to convincing Galloway he had a psycho on his hands. If Daniel didn’t get out soon, he wouldn’t be able to hold it together. That time was coming closer every second.

His gut filled with panic until one mind-blowing thought intruded. Raven was vulnerable, and he couldn’t help her from in here—or from the psycho ward.

He’d tried not to let her get to him.

Who was he kidding? She already had.

Daniel gritted his teeth, sat up and stared through the bars, clenching and reclenching his fists, his knuckles turning white. His hands were clammy, and he fought the urge to rock in place. He rubbed his wrists. At least the sheriff had finally removed the cuffs. Just in time. Daniel had been ready to throttle Galloway to get the keys.

He hadn't done it. He'd maintained control.

Barely.

When the bars had clanked closed, the crisscross of scars on Daniel's back had started to burn. He'd promised himself he'd never be in this situation again. Never be incarcerated. Never be captive and powerless again.

He wiped the sweat from his eyes, restless, edgy, like he was jumping out of his skin. He should have left Raven at the clinic and moved on. He didn't even know her. She was none of his business.

An image of her pain-filled eyes haunted him, though, hitting him harder than the echoes of remembered screams in his mind. Stronger than the memory of his torturer's laughter. The snap of the whip. The sound of bones breaking. Those were all trumped by Raven's small whimper of pain and the way she'd looked at him with such trust.

Good God, lady, don't depend on me.

Unable to sit still any longer, Daniel rose and grabbed the cold steel bars and shook them, testing the lock. Nothing gave at all. He was trapped. Trapped again. He crumpled to his knees, unable to fight his demons anymore. His fingers ached from gripping the bars, and an animal sound of terror rose within him.

His shoulders shook, and he struggled not to break. Not that it mattered anymore.

The other cells were empty.

"Help me, Lord," Daniel prayed. "Don't let me crack. *Don't let me become like my father.*"

The doorknob separating the sheriff's office from the jail twisted.

Daniel stood swiftly, bracing himself to bear his full weight, despite his legs shaking. He froze his emotions inside, hoping his face had gone blank.

The sheriff stepped inside and stared at Daniel.

Galloway leaned his shoulder on the jamb, his relaxed stance feigned. Daniel recognized the tension in the guy's body. Militarylike awareness. Maybe Special Forces.

"Well, Adams, Milly at the diner verified your identity as someone she served yesterday—solo. Said you were a *lone* handyman looking for work. She didn't have anything for you, so she sent you down the north county road to ask at one of the ranches on the outskirts of town."

Daniel shifted his feet, the urge to shake the bars nearly overwhelming, so he just nodded.

Galloway rested his hand on his gun. "I also had a very interesting conversation with Blake Redmond, the sheriff in Carder, Texas, who said he knows all about you."

"Fantastic." Even a good friend like Blake couldn't have vouched for him with all the rumors flowing during Daniel's disappearance. He'd been called traitor until he'd been rescued from his captivity, and now he'd just gone for a walk—across the country. Blake could very well have told Galloway to throw away the key.

"Actually, in your situation, it is. The man vouched for you. Said you're a lot more than a regular handyman. Said you possess some serious skills in a lot of areas. Not that I'm surprised. Your whole vibe says ex-military or mercenary. Doesn't necessarily say sane."

Daniel gritted his teeth.

The sheriff crossed one boot over the other. "I know men like you, Adams. I know about the nightmares. The panicked look when you're trapped in a cell." He strode over to the door and yanked out an impressive set of keys. "I'm letting you go—"

Daniel's heart slammed in his chest.

"—but there's a condition."

Daniel stared down the sheriff. "Name it."

"There are no missing person reports filed on Raven, or Jane Doe, or whoever the hell she is. Milly swears you couldn't have had supper at the diner and made it to the mine fast enough to hurt the woman. Now me? I'm harder to convince, but my gut says it's not you."

Galloway stood with the key in his hand, just inches from the lock. Daniel's breath caught. *Open the damn door.*

The sheriff turned the key in the barred door. "But, Adams, I think you should keep drifting through. Just because my town's name is Trouble doesn't mean I ask for it. And something about you smells like trouble."

Daniel walked through the cell door, not letting Galloway see his enormous relief or his shaking hands. He grabbed his duffel bag off the floor from where Galloway had tossed it earlier. Daniel slung it over his shoulder, then turned to the sheriff.

"Whether you believe me or not, Raven is in serious danger. Somebody left her to die. She couldn't have escaped on her own." If it hadn't been for Trouble, she might never have been found. She wouldn't have survived. The thought made him shudder. "I hope you're better than good at your job, because when the killer discovers she's alive, he'll track her down."

Galloway nodded. "She'll be taken care of."

"Because if something happens to her, I'll—"

Galloway stilled, his stance poised and coiled like a dangerous animal. "You'll do what, Adams?"

"I'll be back to find out why," Daniel warned.

Just then a skinny young man slammed into the room,

his cheeks red, huffing and puffing. His new uniform, creased pants and bit of peach fuzz on his chin screamed *rookie.*

"Sheriff." The nervous deputy skidded to a halt in front of Galloway. "Sheriff, that Jane Doe from the hospital… someone just tried to strangle her."

LIGHTS FLASHED THROUGH the night sky, and the siren rang out. The few people on the streets of Trouble turned their heads to stare as the sheriff's car raced by. This time Daniel rode in the front seat.

"You said she was safe," Daniel accused, his biting words cold as he attempted to tamp down the fury building in his gut.

"I didn't expect someone to attack her in the middle of the emergency room," Galloway snapped.

"You're paid to expect the worst. She should never have been left alone."

Galloway yanked the steering wheel hard to the right, and the car squealed into the parking lot.

Daniel leaped out and ran toward the building, despite the pain in his leg. He raced inside the clinic, to the desk. "Where is she?" he demanded. "Where's Jane Doe?"

The shaking nurse pointed to the same examining room Raven had been in before. Daniel flung aside the wall of fabric, the squeal of the curtain rings barely registering this time. "Raven!"

She lay on the bed, her eyes closed. Bruises encircled her neck.

At the sight, rage erupted in his gut.

He sat down next to her and gently touched her hand. "Oh, darlin'. I never should have let the sheriff take me."

Raven's eyelids fluttered open, then her eyes widened. "Daniel."

He scarcely recognized the raw, hoarse voice she used.

"Daniel, you're here." She clasped hold of his hand. "Don't leave me, please. He almost killed me."

"I won't," he promised. "Not until you're safe." Whoever had attacked her had come too close to cracking her voice box. "I'll be right by your side."

He glared at Sheriff Galloway, daring him to challenge Daniel's vow.

The man gave a slight nod and stepped behind the curtain.

"Thank you. I'm sorry about before." She closed her eyes. "I'm so glad you're here…" Her voice trailed off in sleep.

Daniel positioned himself as best he could to watch over her until the shuddering left her and her breathing steadied into the rhythm of sleep. He eased the still-tight grip of her hand, then stalked to just beyond the curtain to where the sheriff stood checking his notes.

Daniel crossed his arms, struggling to stay civil. "Well?"

"No one saw him come in. From what Raven relayed to the staff, someone dressed as a doctor tried to choke her. He appeared to be acting alone. She fought back and must have hit him just right. She probably broke his nose, and he ran out. Nearly took out the doc and the crash cart."

"You get samples of his blood?" Daniel asked.

"Yes, and I can send them to Midland for forensics, but unless the guy is in one of the government databases, we're not going to be able to identify him. As it is, it's gonna take a while for the results."

Daniel gave the sheriff a sidelong glance. "What if I told you I had contacts with serious forensic resources? Would you give me a blood specimen?"

"These 'contacts' of yours could fast-track it?" Galloway's brow arched.

Daniel nodded. "They can hit all the federal databases a hell of a lot faster than your lab. And they're certified. You can use the results for the court case."

The sheriff paused for a moment, his gaze settling on Raven's bruised throat and head wound. "I'll get you a second sample. We keep this between us."

Daniel agreed, then studied the small emergency department. Double doors leading to hospital rooms, a few cabinets and a second triage area. Only two or three staff members that he could see. "How'd the perp know Raven was here?"

The sheriff grimaced. "Local news picked up the story after I called into the clinic to say we were on our way. We don't get that many emergency calls around here. A few illegals who chose a bad stretch of border to cross, some domestic disturbances and the occasional drunk driver. Can't sneeze in this town without someone knowing about it."

"Great." Daniel swore again silently. "If this story has hit the news, you'll need a guard on her 24/7. Right now whoever attacked her has all the advantages."

"I know you're right, but no can do," Galloway said. "I'm down one man already, with half the damn county to cover. That's nearly two thousand square miles. Even if I could spare the deputy I have left, he can't watch her nonstop."

"I wouldn't let you put that prepubescent kid on her, anyway. He couldn't protect her from a puppy, much less a killer."

Galloway crossed his arms. "I can stick her in jail for her own protection."

Daniel's entire body tensed at the idea of Raven surrounded by bars. "She didn't do anything wrong."

"At least she'd be safe."

"How do you know?" Daniel challenged. "If you can't guard her in the clinic, how can you guard her in the jail? Someone wants her dead. All he'd have to do is create a diversion pulling you two away from the station, and you'd be leaving her vulnerable."

Galloway tilted his head. "So we're at an impasse. I don't have the manpower. I don't have the money. Unless..." He stared at Daniel for a long moment.

"Unless what?"

"Unless you really are some whizbang hotshot military type. Sheriff Redmond said you're handy with tools a lot more lethal than a hammer and nails. And you're one of the best trackers and investigators money can buy."

"Blake Redmond should learn to keep his mouth shut."

"He was trying to save your butt from an attempted murder charge. Kissing his feet is the least you could do." Galloway paused. "Seriously, as you so delicately pointed out, I could use the help on this one. The doctor said Raven has traumatic amnesia. Her memory may or may not return. Until we know better, we have nothing else to go on except whatever clues come out of that mine."

"And the blood sample from her attacker," Daniel pointed out.

"That, too," the sheriff agreed. "But, like you said, she needs someone protecting her 24/7. How about it? I could deputize you."

"That's a switch. An hour ago, you were running me out of town."

"Yeah, well, things change. I just need your signature on a form, and you have to take a quick oath."

Daniel looked back at the curtain behind which Raven slept. He'd promised he wouldn't leave her until she was safe. He couldn't let her fight this alone. Someone had tried to kill her twice. Daniel didn't have a choice, and Galloway knew it. "I have your resources available to me?"

"Whatever you need, though you may have more than I do."

"Your name makes the request more…official. And just so we're clear, this isn't a permanent assignment, Sheriff. You understand that? Once I find out who's after Raven, I'm back on the road."

"You won't hear me complaining. I want my quiet town back."

"If I need more help—more manpower from my contacts—can I make a few calls?"

"Exactly what are you saying?"

"I won't get any flack for bringing outsiders into your county?"

The sheriff shot him a speculative glance. "Does Sheriff Redmond also know these mysterious *resources?*"

"Most definitely. Feel free to call him to check them out."

"Just what are these 'outsiders' going to do?"

"I know people who can look in a lot of gray areas with finesse and speed," Daniel replied easily. "Their only goal is justice."

The men's gazes met. They understood each other.

"I won't look the other way, Adams, if you go beyond the law…that is, if I know about it," Galloway said.

Daniel rolled the sheriff's comments around in his mind. So Galloway believed in justice more than rules. Daniel's kind of law enforcement. "Understood."

Galloway signaled his deputy, who had brought Daniel's duffel into the clinic. "I left your Glock in there. I imagine you know how to use it. You require anything else?"

Daniel shook his head at the dig. "I have what I need."

"Then I'll set up the paperwork for you to sign."

Daniel gave Galloway a nod, then eased aside the curtain and walked over to Raven's bed. After setting down his pack, he unzipped the duffel, pulled his Glock from its case and checked the magazine. Everything seemed set. With calm precision, he tucked the weapon in the back of his jeans, then yanked his knife and ankle sheath from the duffel's side pocket. After one quick buckle of the sheath's strap around his leg, Daniel was able to slip in his knife. Relieved at having his two primary weapons within easy reach, he settled down to wait.

It was odd that being in the tight enclosure in the examining room didn't seem as bad now. Almost as if the fact that he was officially guarding someone nullified some of the usual discomforts of small places. Of course, it helped that the walls were made of cotton, not stone.

The next two hours sitting on a hard wooden chair didn't help Daniel's leg. He adjusted his position, but he couldn't get comfortable. At least the twinges kept him awake.

Not that he hadn't been mesmerized by the rise and fall of Raven's chest or the temptation of her full lips as they parted with each breath, but the shadows under her eyes reminded him of the danger stalking her and exactly why he was here.

The curtain at the end of her bed shifted slightly. Daniel tensed. He palmed the Glock and held it at his side.

The fabric parted. A woman in pink scrubs stepped through. Daniel hid the weapon from her sight as the nurse checked Raven's vital signs.

"How is she doing?" Daniel whispered.

"Everything seems normal."

"What about her memory?"

The woman's sympathetic look evoked an ache deep in Daniel's chest. He didn't want his concern for Raven to be so obvious. He was just worried about her safety.

None of this was personal.

It couldn't be.

His recent stint in the jail cell had shown him just how messed up he truly was. He wouldn't saddle anyone with that crap to deal with for life. Been there. Done that. Had his father's spent bullet casing from his suicide to show for it. Daniel wouldn't put anyone through that.

The nurse checked the IV needle before turning back to Daniel. "The doctor said her memory could come back anytime—or not at all," she said. "She has a concussion, and he wants to keep her for observation."

"Isn't there a quieter location we could stay? A private room maybe? Away from everyone else?" *Especially murdering psychos.*

"I'm sorry. The clinic only has a dozen beds. They're all taken," she said. "This will have to do until something comes available."

Not good enough. Daniel wanted security, minimal entrances and exits. And distance. As it was, three-quarters of this room could be moved with a harsh breath to the fabric curtain. Besides, the perp knew her location. Nowhere in this clinic was safe.

"Does she have to stay in the hospital tonight? I've had enough concussions to know the drill. I'll check her status every hour, and I can bring her back if there are changes, but I need to take her somewhere more secure."

The nurse frowned. "I'll contact her physician. After what happened earlier, I understand your concern."

"Is there a hotel nearby?"

"There's a *motel,* the Copper Mine, just at the edge of town. Run by a bit of a character, but Hondo keeps a clean place."

Daniel chewed on his lip, not liking the idea of sleeping indoors, but at least in a motel room he had a chance to protect Raven. One entrance and solid walls. “Thanks for the tip.”

The nurse left, and he pulled out his cell phone, powering the thing on for the first time since leaving the mine. He still had battery life—and twenty-four messages, since he hadn’t bothered to listen to them in the past month.

He ignored the voice mails and stared once more at Raven lying on the bed. Who was she really? What was her name? Who wanted her dead?

He put in a call to Galloway’s office requesting a list of missing persons reported in Texas and New Mexico. Galloway, apparently a man of his word, sent Daniel the information quickly to his phone. After a quick review of the small number of cases and watching the room’s TV for any updates, he let out a sigh.

Nothing. The local television story on Raven hadn’t hit the national news or even the big affiliates. At this point Daniel wished it had. Since the person who had buried Raven in that mine knew she was still alive, they were playing against time. More extensive news coverage might give them her name.

His gaze swept Raven’s still body. How could no one be missing her? Then again, maybe she was a loner. Some people didn’t reach out, didn’t create spheres of friends. Some people were totally on their own. Might be nice on occasion. Daniel had tried to disappear, and no one would let him.

A glint of gold around Raven’s neck flickered under the fluorescent light. Daniel leaned forward in his chair and tugged on the chain, pulling the heart-shaped locket free of her hospital johnny.

He shifted closer in his seat and palmed the locket, the necklace she had clutched with such desperation. Maybe there were clues inside. His fingernail pressed the latch and opened the heart.

"What are you doing?" she asked groggily, her voice still raspy.

Her cinnamon-colored eyes opened, and he nearly drowned in them.

He gave her a small smile, relieved she'd regained consciousness. "Checking out your necklace." He ran a gentle finger down the smooth skin at her temple. "Trying to find out who you are," Daniel said softly.

She glanced at the small heart locket he'd opened. "Is that a picture inside?"

"Yes, of a raven-haired baby, and a lock of hair tied with a pink ribbon," Daniel said. "Recognize her?"

Raven sat up, her hand trembling as she studied the picture.

"Do you think it's me as a baby? It's my hair. Or could my dream be real?" she whispered. "What if that pink blanket and that poor baby's cry are memories?"

She rubbed her upper arms with her hands as if warding off a chill; then she stared at him, dread lacing her gaze. "Could the person who tried to kill me have taken my baby girl?"

NIGHT IN TROUBLE, Texas, hid a man and his bloody nose well. A few streetlights, a few houselights, but Christopher could disappear in this small town. He was good at disappearing and not being seen as he went about his business.

His footsteps pounded the pavement, the rhythm a little slower now. He sucked in a few breaths. He could do this. The run wasn't nearly as tough as in boot camp. In fact, he'd feel great if it weren't for his broken nose.

God, he wanted that woman dead. He couldn't believe she'd done this to him. She barely weighed as much as his duffel bag from Afghanistan, but she packed a helluva punch. He hadn't expected that, and now he was on the run, covered with blood, wearing stolen clothes and stealing down dark streets to get back to his car.

All because of that bitch.

He heard the sound of not-so-distant laughter and took off again. Alley after alley, corner after corner on foot.

He rounded another dark turn, leaned back against a cinder-block wall and tilted his head to hold his nose at the bridge, knowing it was a bad bone break, and he'd have to be careful until it healed.

If the woman had known a little bit more about what she was doing, he'd be dead. Apparently she'd taken enough self-defense training to do damage. A little harder, a slightly different angle and shards of bone would have sliced up into his brain. He'd have dropped on the spot. The fact that he was in a medical clinic at the time wouldn't have saved him.

Two sets of sirens blasted into the night. Christopher shrank into the blackness. They wouldn't find him.

This whole situation pissed him off. This was *not* how he'd planned his welcome home.

His mom had panicked when that news report had come on. His emotions had taken over. He knew better. He never should have let his mother influence his plans.

Yeah, he liked killing, but he hadn't taken the time to study the layout. He'd be lucky if that fiasco at the clinic didn't put his butt in a sling. They probably had security cameras. He'd screwed up and given too much away about himself. He rubbed his thumb along the barrel of his HK, almost wishing he'd used the gun instead of trying to strangle her.

He wouldn't make the same mistake again.

But they'd be watching her now, closely. He needed the

element of surprise and a bit of help. Someone who understood the stakes and the joys of a good kill.

Christopher untucked his cell phone from his pocket and dialed his buddy's number. "Pick up, you loser."

Ring after ring. Just as he was about to give up, Tad answered.

"This better be good, or you're in a serious world of hurt," the voice at the other end muttered, sleep clogging the words.

"Wake up, you lazy slug. Wanna go hunting?"

Christopher could almost see his ex-platoon-mate's face perk up in interest. "I'm listening and assuming you're not talking about quail."

"I have a woman who needs to disappear. For good. Get my drift?"

"Chelsea?"

"No, I haven't even seen her yet. It's someone you don't know."

"No rules?"

"Just help me make her go away."

"What's the lucky lady's name?"

"That's the best part. She hasn't got one, and I'd kinda like to keep it that way."

Chapter Four

Daniel didn't know how long he had waited for Raven's breathing to even out in deep sleep. He eased the curtain closed and walked across the room. Sheriff Galloway stood whispering with the doctor.

"You checking up on me, Sheriff?"

"Always."

"You know I can handle this. Or are you here to kick me out of town again for some reason?"

"I have an investigation to follow up." Galloway gave Daniel an irritated glance. "You have *your* job. How's she doing?"

"She finally fell asleep. Raven can't remember anything, but she thinks she might have a baby out there."

Galloway stilled. "What the hell… We have a missing baby on top of everything else?"

"I don't know." Daniel described the locket. "The truth is, I have no idea if she's remembering something or not. She doesn't know, either. All I can tell you is that her only memories are of a pink blanket and hearing a baby cry."

The sheriff thrust his hand through his hair. "Nothing's hit my radar. Damn it." Galloway looked at the doctor. "Has she had a baby? Can we tell?"

The doctor shifted uncomfortably under the sheriff's gaze.

"Could Raven have a baby out there?" Daniel glared. "The attacker may have her."

The man cleared his throat and shifted his feet, then finally let out a long breath. "Since Raven doesn't have a memory, and there might be a child at risk…I can reveal that she has given birth. I can't tell you when. Only that it wasn't recent."

Galloway grabbed his phone and made a call. "I want a search statewide on missing children over the past two weeks. See if anyone reported a mother *and* child missing. And check on the status of Jane Doe's prints. I need to know who she is." His expression turned deadly as he listened. "No, it can't wait until morning." He snapped the phone closed and faced the doctor. "What else can we do?"

"Not much, until she remembers."

"How long will that be?" Daniel asked.

"I wish I could tell you. We know a lot about the human body, but the brain is one organ that I'm sorry to say is, in many ways, a mystery. She has a traumatic brain injury even though the MRI doesn't show any swelling. Honestly there doesn't appear to be any physical reason she shouldn't remember."

Daniel paced back and forth. "That's not good enough. She needs to remember—for her own safety as well as the baby's—so how can we speed up the process?"

"Look, *Deputy,* you can't force a brain that's been injured to work on a timetable. And we have no idea what happened to her out there. Her body is protecting her right now. We have to let her heal."

Daniel lifted his gaze to the ceiling. "This is crazy. Every hour we delay is more time for her attacker to try again."

"And the harder you push, the more she may bury the memories until they never come back." The doctor narrowed his gaze at Daniel. "I know you're impatient. I'm concerned about the baby, too, but I'm more concerned about the patient who I know exists. You have to go slowly."

"You're giving me nothing, doc."

"Maybe if you retrace her steps, the familiar *might* bring something back. *If* this isn't all in her imagination. Scent is also a strong trigger. Get some baby lotion or shampoo and introduce it naturally, with no expectations. She'll remember more. Other than that, she needs rest and no stress."

Daniel glanced back at the closed curtain. "That I can do. I can keep her safe and calm," he said quietly. "She will remember." Daniel pinned the sheriff with his gaze. "My gut tells me there is a child. Raven's reaction was visceral. It was the first thing she said when she woke up. Can you use your network to find out if the baby exists?"

Galloway nodded. "I'm on it."

"I'll protect Raven. The perp obviously knows she's here. She can't stay."

The sheriff's phone rang. "Galloway."

As the person on the other end spoke, the sheriff's jawline went tense. "Keep digging. She didn't come out of nowhere."

He ended the call.

"No leads?" Daniel asked.

"Her prints didn't get a hit. Nothing on the missing persons reports that matches her or a dark-haired child of any age. We've got squat."

"How does a woman—and perhaps a child—vanish without anyone reporting it? Something's not right." Daniel thrust his hand into his pocket and worried the bullet casing.

Galloway nodded. "Her husband—"

"She's not wearing a ring," Daniel said harshly. He

pounced on the statement. He didn't want anyone to be in Raven's life. No one but him.

His fingers flicked against the brass's metal edge. That was wrong. He knew better than to let himself get involved. He could hurt her. She was simply a woman who needed help, but somehow, over the past few hours, she'd become important to him. More important than she should.

"Husband or not, every baby has a father. Most of the time child abduction is a family member, typically a parent. We have to consider the father the prime suspect."

"Except we don't know her identity. Or his. Or even if there *is* an abduction. Until we know who Raven is, we have no leads."

"Catch twenty-two," Galloway muttered.

"Doesn't matter. She's still in danger. I'm taking her out of here," Daniel said. "When can she leave?" he asked the doctor.

Daniel wanted to grab her and get her away from this place. Even as he looked around the waiting room, all he saw were opportunities for an attack. Numerous entrances and easy access.

"Tomorrow." The doctor stroked his jaw. "I can't do anything else for her, but she has a concussion. I want her here for the remainder of the night just in case of complications. I'll check her again first thing in the morning. If she doesn't have further symptoms, you can take her, but you'll need to watch her closely. If she gets nauseous or dizzy or starts seeing double again, bring her back in."

Daniel's body tensed in resistance. She was open and vulnerable here. This was a bad idea. He could feel it. He opened his mouth to argue—

"I'm not backing down," the doctor said. "If she takes a turn for the worse, she'll need immediate medical intervention."

"In the meantime, I want all staff to deny Raven's presence here. Got it?" Daniel told the doc.

He received a nod in return from the physician.

A loud ruckus outside the hospital interrupted the discussion. Daniel whirled around, hand on his weapon. A television news crew pushed their way into the emergency room lobby. Daniel glared at the sheriff and whirled behind the curtain hiding Raven, letting him and the doc deal with the intrusion.

After several minutes of heated argument, the sheriff got rid of the news crew. Galloway stuck his head through the curtain and nodded. "Doc's distracting them in the parking lot."

With a last check on the woman who hadn't regained consciousness even in the turmoil, Daniel stalked back into the emergency room's lobby. "We leave in the morning. Until then, I'll take watch." He turned to the sheriff and, after a quick look around verifying no one was eavesdropping, lowered his voice. "I hear there's a decent motel at the edge of town. Any reason for us not to stay there?"

"I'll call Hondo," Galloway offered, his voice lowered, as well. "The guy's discreet and knows his way around a weapon or two. If Raven feels safe enough, like the doc said, maybe she'll remember."

"A motel is better than fabric walls. But I still want to see the place before she goes anywhere near the joint."

Galloway took out his phone. "I'll make the arrangements."

"Keep it quiet, Sheriff. I don't like how much this guy knows."

With a quick nod and agreement to return at dawn to watch Raven while Daniel checked out the motel, Galloway left.

Daniel stepped back through the curtain protecting

Raven. Shadows marred her pale complex
stop staring at the porcelain of her skin
bility of her expression. Her full lips ha
but they turned down at the corners, her
on her face. He could understand that.
centimeters from the skin he knew wo
a breath of fresh air.

He closed his fist and pulled away.
than he would ever be. That bullet in
reminder that not everyone made it b

With a sigh, he settled into the c
bed. Anyone looking in would think
a chance. Her fear-filled eyes haunte

But no one would get near Raven

Not on his watch.

CHRISTOPHER GINGERLY PRESSED ag
He swore and scanned the eerily
the alley behind the sheriff's offi
of the phone line coming down th

Thank God this decrepit town
tem in decades.

"This is stupid," Tad hissed.
caught?"

"You a coward?" Christoph
knew what buttons to push w
an accomplice, but this was cl
topher had to stay out of sigh
needed backup.

No one better than the gu
gotten thrown in jail togeth
gether and had found a way
tary together.

Christopher could count

"In the meantime, I want all staff to deny Raven's presence here. Got it?" Daniel told the doc.

He received a nod in return from the physician.

A loud ruckus outside the hospital interrupted the discussion. Daniel whirled around, hand on his weapon. A television news crew pushed their way into the emergency room lobby. Daniel glared at the sheriff and whirled behind the curtain hiding Raven, letting him and the doc deal with the intrusion.

After several minutes of heated argument, the sheriff got rid of the news crew. Galloway stuck his head through the curtain and nodded. "Doc's distracting them in the parking lot."

With a last check on the woman who hadn't regained consciousness even in the turmoil, Daniel stalked back into the emergency room's lobby. "We leave in the morning. Until then, I'll take watch." He turned to the sheriff and, after a quick look around verifying no one was eavesdropping, lowered his voice. "I hear there's a decent motel at the edge of town. Any reason for us not to stay there?"

"I'll call Hondo," Galloway offered, his voice lowered, as well. "The guy's discreet and knows his way around a weapon or two. If Raven feels safe enough, like the doc said, maybe she'll remember."

"A motel is better than fabric walls. But I still want to see the place before she goes anywhere near the joint."

Galloway took out his phone. "I'll make the arrangements."

"Keep it quiet, Sheriff. I don't like how much this guy knows."

With a quick nod and agreement to return at dawn to watch Raven while Daniel checked out the motel, Galloway left.

Daniel stepped back through the curtain protecting

Raven. Shadows marred her pale complexion. He couldn't stop staring at the porcelain of her skin or the vulnerability of her expression. Her full lips had parted slightly, but they turned down at the corners, her troubles painted on her face. He could understand that. His hand hovered centimeters from the skin he knew would be softer than a breath of fresh air.

He closed his fist and pulled away. She deserved better than he would ever be. That bullet in his pocket was his reminder that not everyone made it back from hell.

With a sigh, he settled into the chair next to Raven's bed. Anyone looking in would think he was relaxed. Not a chance. Her fear-filled eyes haunted his memory.

But no one would get near Raven again.

Not on his watch.

CHRISTOPHER GINGERLY PRESSED against his swollen nose. He swore and scanned the eerily quiet surroundings in the alley behind the sheriff's office before catching sight of the phone line coming down the side of the building.

Thank God this decrepit town hadn't updated the system in decades.

"This is stupid," Tad hissed. "Are you trying to get us caught?"

"You a coward?" Christopher egged on his friend. He knew what buttons to push with Tad. He hadn't wanted an accomplice, but this was clearly a two-man job. Christopher had to stay out of sight until his nose healed. He needed backup.

No one better than the guy he'd grown up with. They'd gotten thrown in jail together, had joined the army together and had found a way to get kicked out of the military together.

Christopher could count on Tad. "Look, the nurse didn't

know anything 'cept Jane Doe left the hospital. If anyone knows where that woman is, it's Sheriff Galloway, and we can't just ask. We need intel."

"I saw the sheriff. Former Special Forces, I bet. He's dangerous. Just like the lieutenant," Tad said.

"We took care of him just fine."

"Yeah, but not quick enough. Still got booted out," Tad grumbled. "No pension, no nothing. Can't even get a frickin' job now. All that time wasted."

"I wouldn't say it was a total waste. I learned a few things and made some pretty good connections." Christopher pulled a small electronic device from his pocket. He clipped it on the phone line that had been tacked to the side of the building and tucked a small earpiece inside in his ear. "Now we'll know exactly what the good sheriff is talking about no matter where we go. When he hears where that woman is, she's dead."

"And what about the sheriff? What if he interferes?"

"If he gets in our way, well, bullets kill Special Forces, too."

THE CLOP OF worn boots sounded on the linoleum floor of the hospital. The owner paused, just visible beneath the curtain. "Come on in, Sheriff," Daniel said, his voice barely above a whisper.

Galloway pressed back the fabric. "You said dawn, so here I am. Any change?"

"The nurse woke Raven about a half hour ago. She seems better."

"Did she remember anything?"

Daniel shook his head and rose.

"I'll watch over her," Galloway said, his hand on his Beretta.

"I won't be long." Daniel paused for a moment and sent

the sheriff a sideways glance. "What are you doing in this Podunk town, Galloway? Something about you doesn't quite fit."

Galloway's lips twisted. "Pot. Kettle."

"Touché," Daniel muttered with one last long glance at the sleeping woman in the bed. He'd teased her about being a sleeping princess, but damned if she didn't fit the part. Just looking at her made his heart ache. "I'll be back, Raven. Count on it."

He shoved aside the unwanted desires. He had to remember the past, the reason he couldn't let himself care. He strode through the small clinic and out the exit. He had a job to do, and nothing, especially not his own weakness, would stop him from protecting her.

The sight greeting him outside the clinic made him shake his head. Trouble. The fuzz face had dust and grime on his coat, but he sat there with a rag in his mouth and expectations on his face.

"What the hell did you get into, boy?" Daniel asked, stepping forward cautiously so as not to run the skittish dog away.

Trouble cocked his head, then dropped his trophy before taking a few steps back to his now customary six feet.

Daniel knelt down, noticing a triangle of material looking like torn jeans. Several red splotches decorated the worn blue fabric. Blood, maybe? "Seems like you had a battle with someone."

His senses pinged with awareness. Raven's attacker had worn jeans. Could he be that lucky? He raced into the hospital and returned wearing a glove on one hand and carrying a bowl of water in the other. Daniel set the liquid down. Trouble didn't hesitate. While the mutt lapped up the drink, Daniel picked up the fabric by the corner, studied it for a moment and dumped it into a paper lunch sack. "Who'd you go after, Trouble?"

He kept his hands by his side, kneeling down, meeting Trouble's gaze at eye level. "You hurt, boy? Will you let me check you over?"

Daniel focused on making his voice calm and smooth. Normally he would've let the dog be, but there was blood on the animal's side.

"I'll be quick." His movements slow and steady, Daniel made more effort than he had in weeks to get close to the dog. As if he understood, Trouble sat quiet but alert. Daniel ran his hands over the mutt's fur.

When he reached the dog's side, Trouble yelped.

"Someone hurt you?" Daniel's gaze hardened, and he palpated the animal's ribs. They didn't seem broken, and there were no cuts, but whoever the canine had attacked had fought back.

"Not too bad. You'll live, boy." Daniel tried to scratch behind the floppy ears, but Trouble's patience had ended. He scooted away.

Daniel stood. "You are one strange dog. I'll drop off your little trophy and see if you tangled with Raven's attacker."

He hurried in and out of the hospital. Trouble hadn't moved. "I'm going for a ride. I don't suppose you want to come?"

Trouble let out a bark. Out of his pocket Daniel pulled the keys to the truck the sheriff had loaned him. The casing from his dad's gun fell to the ground. Daniel scooped it up. He couldn't lose the reminder. That mutt, and now Raven, had somehow embedded themselves behind the protective wall Daniel had constructed around his heart. All he had to do was look at the cylinder of brass to remind him of what he'd come home to that horrible afternoon.

Blood and brains splattered on the wall of his father's bedroom. His sisters' screams when they'd followed him into that death room.

He shook his head to dispel the memories. No time for the past.

With a quick tug he opened the door of the truck. "Well?"

He half expected Trouble to skedaddle, but the dog surprised him yet again. He jumped into the vehicle and sat on the passenger seat.

"So you hate cop cars and uniforms, do you, but not trucks? I can't say that I blame you. Just takes one psycho in uniform to sour the taste."

Daniel put the truck into gear and exited the hospital parking lot. Trouble stuck his head out the window, letting the wind blow through his reddish hair, with that crazy dog smile on his face. The trip didn't last long, though. Within a few minutes, Daniel had traveled from one end of the small town to the other.

He pulled inside the parking lot of the Copper Mine Motel. The place should have been a dump, but a fresh coat of paint brightened it up, and two iron kettles of pansies lined each side of the screen door entrance, giving it a vintage and welcoming vibe.

Daniel pressed the buzzer.

A curtain pushed aside. A tiny woman with scraggly gray hair and piercing blue eyes peeped through the gap. "You Daniel Adams?"

"Don't be asking him his name, Lucy. How many times have I told you, you give away too much? What if it's a bad guy?"

She pouted, then shrugged. "How many visitors we get at the crack of dawn? Besides, I can spot a bad guy a mile away. Quit babying me, big brother. You're not my keeper."

A large barrel-chested man opened the door. His brown hair was wild, but his beard well kempt. Tattoos covered his arms. A steel loop pierced his lip.

Incongruously, oven mitts encased his hands, and he held a fresh-baked pan of chocolate chip cookies. “Sorry for the delay. Had to get these out of the oven.”

So not a picture Daniel had expected. The cookies should belong to his sister. This guy should be greased up, taking a wrench to a Harley. “You're Hondo?”

“You got it. This is my place.”

His sister cleared her throat and glared at him.

“Yeah, well, Lucy here got it in a settlement from her lyin', cheatin' ex-husband.” He glanced at his sister. “But I'm the one who keeps the place from falling down around your feet. Isn't that right, little sister?”

“Just don't you forget who's in charge,” she huffed. “I'm going to watch wrestling.”

“Keep the volume down,” he commented with a smile in his eyes. He turned back to Daniel. “She's far too trusting. I hear you need a room.”

“For a while.”

“I also hear you prefer no record that you're staying here,” he said with a scowl. “I don't want no problems. I see any funny business goin' on, I won't hesitate to call the sheriff. I'm only lettin' you stay 'cause he vouched for you.”

“Agreed.” Daniel pulled out his wallet.

Hondo raised his hand. “Sheriff took care of one week's rent. We'll talk after that if we're both still interested.”

Daniel studied the man in front of him. He didn't see deception behind Hondo's eyes. “That's fair.” He shoved his billfold back into his pocket. “One week.”

“Good.” Hondo smiled and held out the baking sheet. “Cookie?”

RAVEN PEERED THROUGH the pickup's window at a succession of mom-and-pop shops down Trouble's main drag and clutched the hospital blanket tighter around her. The big stores hadn't invaded yet. A few doorways had been blockaded, but for the most part, this little Texas town looked to be doing all right. Better than she was, certainly.

She shivered, then huddled against the truck's worn seats. Despite the temperatures in the seventies outside, she couldn't stop the chills from skittering down her arms. She clutched at Trouble's fur. His big brown eyes peered up at her from his spot on the floorboard. The dog could very well be the only reason her legs had stayed warm. He didn't want to move away from her. She appreciated the loyalty.

"I can't believe he's letting you pet him like that," Daniel muttered.

Raven scratched Trouble's floppy ears. "I like dogs. And he's well trained. A service dog, do you think?"

"Maybe," Daniel said. "He didn't have any tags, and he doesn't act like a K-9, but I gotta wonder if he might be search and rescue after watching him find you in that mine. He wouldn't stop until I dug you out."

She lifted Trouble's chin. "So, boy, you're a smart one, aren't you? You saved my life." The animal tilted his head into her touch, and she fondled his soft ears and bent down. "Thank you," she whispered.

Daniel pulled the truck into the parking lot of a motel and turned off the keys. "This place should be safer than the hospital."

She peered at the newly polished sign. *Copper Mine Motel.* Her fingers explored the bruises on her throat that the attacker had made. "I'm not sure if I should be relieved or worried."

After Daniel turned off the engine, he twisted in his seat, his gaze intense, his expression unrelenting. "Even if your attacker finds us, there's only one entrance. He'll have to go through me and Trouble to get at you. We won't let that happen." He touched her arm lightly. "I promise you that."

His words made her want to believe, to put herself into his hands. She couldn't do this alone. If she'd been totally alone throughout this whole ordeal, she would be dead right now. Of that she had no doubt. She nodded at Daniel, regretting the action the moment her chin bobbed down. She could almost feel her brain banging against her skull. Even though the pain meds had taken the edge off, she could still sense every small movement from her neck up.

She winced, and he must have caught it.

"You're hurting again," Daniel said. He opened the door and stepped outside. "Stay here. I'll be right back."

He walked a few feet across the porch and knocked on the side jamb. A huge, scary-looking man stood in the doorway. Raven tensed, her gut winding in a knot. Trouble whimpered and laid his head in her lap. She gripped his fur and reached toward the door. She didn't have a plan, but she couldn't let Daniel fight the big man alone. If nothing else, she could be a distraction.

Then the mountain smiled, tilted back his head and chuckled. He slapped Daniel across the back and disappeared inside.

Daniel looked toward her and offered her a reassuring nod. He scanned the surroundings, and she knew he kept watch for her. Raven sagged in the seat and leaned her head against the soft back, uncertain why she'd been expecting an attack. The bright blue of the morning sky didn't appear real. Nothing did. Gingerly she ran her finger along the bandage still covering the cut on her head. She pressed gently against the injury. A sharp stab of pain needled her temple.

At least the pain proved this wasn't some crazy dream.

She was real. The locket was real. She snapped opened the catch. Was the baby real, too?

Searching for something to ground her, she let her gaze wander, looking for anything familiar. She could identify the steering wheel; she recognized the windmill looming above the motel. Her gaze swept the motel sign again. Copper.

The symbol for the element was *Cu.*

Her heart fluttered. She looked around. Where had *that* come from?

The wrought iron windmill. Iron, *Fe.*

She clutched her locket. Gold, *Au.*

Her head ached, but an almost desperate excitement rose within her. She *knew* this information. The knowledge was second nature. She could identify the elements clearly, easily. Was she a chemistry teacher? A scientist?

She glanced at the cantina across the road. Drinking alcohol, ethyl alcohol or ethyl hydroxide. *EtOH.* Flash point: pure EtOH caught fire at just under seventeen degrees centigrade.

She grabbed Trouble's fur. "I remember something from before."

Daniel opened her door. "We're in room number six," he said.

She barely heard him, digging her fingers into his arm. "I know the periodic table of the elements. I know chemicals. Benzene. C6H6. An organic chemical compound. A natural constituent of crude oil. It has a sweet smell." Her body shook. "It's like breathing air. I know it the same way I know Trouble is a dog, and you're a man, and that knob turns on the radio."

She smiled up at him. "My head hurts like the devil, but I know my chemistry."

"Chemistry," Daniel muttered. "It's a good start." He slid his hands under her and swept her into his arms, then glanced around. "You can tell me all about it once we're inside."

"I'm too heavy," she protested.

"I carried you a couple miles down that highway," he said, tightening his grip. "I'm getting used to the feel of you in my arms."

Daniel balanced her against his chest, and she couldn't help feeling small against his broad shoulders. He was a bit lean for his build, as if he hadn't eaten right, but every sinew of muscle oozed strength.

With a quick turn of an old key, he pushed into the motel room. Trouble bounded in ahead of them, checking out the place, his nose against the carpet.

Daniel's arms tightened around her as if he didn't want to let her go. His gaze dropped to her mouth, and suddenly the sheer joy of knowledge transformed into something else. His eyes grew dark, a flicker of green sparking in the hazel depths. Her breath caught. She was hurt, dusty and so not-sexy, but she couldn't help but lean into him. In the uncertainty of her current existence, he had become a constant.

Her hands flattened on his strong shoulders. His fingers moved along her back, and a flash of awareness tingled through her. Her lungs tightened, and her mouth went dry. She wet her lower lip, and his chest rumbled against hers.

Sparks she recognized ignited between them, and she squirmed.

In two steps Daniel laid her on the regular-sized bed taking over the room. His movements gentle, he placed a pillow behind her back.

She looked to the other side of the mattress, clutching the simple quilt with her fingertips. Not much room.

If he wanted to sleep in the bed with her, they couldn't help touching each other. Her gaze lifted to his, and she bit her lip.

The heat in Daniel's gaze dimmed, and he took in a shuddering breath, as if fighting for control. He doused the fire burning between them and took a step back. "Sorry. They didn't have a room with two beds available." Daniel placed his hand on her arm, his touch reigniting that shiver of awareness she couldn't deny. She may not know her name, but she knew the electricity sparking between them didn't happen often.

He snatched his hand back from her arm. "We need to lay down some ground rules. You don't answer the phone or the door. You don't stand by the windows. You let me enter first wherever we go. Got it?"

"But—"

"It's not negotiable, darlin'. You sleep here, as far away from the door as possible while I'm keeping watch by the window. You don't have to be afraid." His face took on a somber expression, and he trailed his finger down her cheek. "Not of anything or anyone."

Including me. He left the unspoken words in the air around them. She shouldn't be afraid of him, and she wasn't, but she couldn't help but be terrified of what she already felt building between them. "I can't let you sleep on the rug."

"It's near the window. I like the open air," he said, his voice soft but certain. "So does Trouble."

Immediately the mutt bounded up on the bed, circled twice and settled on top of Raven's feet. His ears flattened, and he stared at Daniel with a *Who me?* expression on his face.

She bit back a small chuckle.

"Traitor." Daniel glared at the dog with a shake of his

head. "I obviously spoke too soon. He's been hanging with me for weeks, and he wouldn't so much as come near. To you, he's pretty much pledged his undying devotion."

Raven scratched Trouble's ears.

"Guard her, Trouble. I'll get our stuff from the truck." He disappeared out the motel room door.

She watched him leave and glanced down at the dog next to her. "Am I fooling myself, boy? Is he really the man he seems to be?"

She wished the animal could answer. Instead, she scanned the small room that would be her home until she remembered her own address. This place had to have been built in the fifties, but the pristine white tile of the bathroom looked new.

What little energy she'd saved had seeped out of her. Her eyelids wanted to close, but she couldn't stand lying down without a shower. She wanted nothing more than to wash the grime off her body, not to mention the blood out of her hair.

Determined to get clean, she swung her legs over the side of the bed and set her feet on the ground.

Daniel came in with his duffel and a grocery sack. "Whoa there. What do you think you're doing?"

"I need a shower." She stood, the back of her knees against the bed.

"Well, it's your lucky day, darlin'. The nurses gathered up a few things for you," he said, lifting the small plastic bag. "Tomorrow I'll try to get you some more clothes. The thing about small towns, there's not always 24/7 retail shopping."

"I don't have any money," she said slowly.

"Don't worry about that. You can pay me back when we find out—"

"You mean *if* we find out who I am," she finished.

"We'll figure it out."

"No one's come forward after the pictures on the news?" Her voice caught, and she wished it hadn't. She didn't like showing vulnerability.

"Not yet."

"How can I just disappear without anyone caring?" She couldn't bear to look at him so she opened the bag and shuffled through the items. Soap, a razor, lotion. Shampoo. She froze. Baby shampoo. She stared at the small bottle for a moment. Compelled, she twisted the cap and took a small sniff. Her head spun a bit, and she sat down quickly.

"Dizzy? Nauseous?" Daniel slipped his phone from his pocket. "I'm calling the doctor."

"It's not that. It's the baby shampoo." She held it up. "I smelled baby lotion in the mine and reacted the same way." Her eyes burned. "It's familiar, Daniel, and my heart feels *so* empty." She looked at the locket. "I know I have a child out there. Somewhere. Needing me."

"Then we'll find her." Daniel knelt at the edge of the bed. He took the small bottle from her and held it to her nose. "Breathe in. Close your eyes. Do you remember anything else?"

Raven let her lashes drop against her cheeks. She took slow, deep breaths, searching her brain for something, anything that would give her an answer.

Only a fog clouded her mind.

"Nothing." She frowned, the sharp words laced with frustration.

He entwined his fingers through hers and squeezed. "Not so fast. Close them again."

She let her eyelids fall. Blackness overtook her vision. Gray shapes swirled. "I see something." A pink blanket. She gripped his hand until her fingers had gone numb. "The blanket again."

"And unicorns," she whispered. "Rainbows and unicorns. It looks like a nursery."

"Okay, that's good. That's very good," Daniel said. "Where?"

The image faded away. She opened her eyes. "I don't know. It was there, but now it's gone."

"Was the light bright? Were you in the west? Here in Texas? Was it cloudy? Maybe Washington or Oregon?" he prompted.

"I don't know. I just don't know." She rubbed the bridge of her nose, then her eyes. Her head pounded with the futile effort.

Raven clutched the small bottle of shampoo and lifted her gaze to Daniel's. "I'm scared for her. I'm safe. I have you to protect me, but the baby's in danger. I can feel it."

A loud pounding at the door jerked Raven from the captivity of Daniel's gaze.

He slipped his Glock from beneath his jacket. "Get out of sight," he hissed. "Now!"

Raven rolled to the side and ducked behind the bed. She peered around the end. Trouble stood beside Daniel, his ears back, a low growl emitting from his throat as he stared intently at the doorknob.

Daniel stood to the side, gun at the ready. He flung open the door. "Don't move, or I'll shoot."

Chapter Five

Pamela gripped the steering wheel of the BMW and stared at the small ranch house situated on an isolated dirt road in the middle of nowhere. She studied the sheet of paper on the seat beside her, the map and phone number in her husband's writing. She'd never thought she'd have to sully her hands again with his less-than-honest *colleagues,* but she needed foolproof documents for her family to disappear out of the system.

She had no choice, not if she wanted to protect them. Her knuckles whitened with tension. A whimper sounded from the backseat. The baby clutched the blanket, her eyes tear-filled.

"You'll be mine soon, little one," she whispered softly. "Forever." She kept the air conditioner running, rolled down the windows and stared at the sweet little girl in the car seat. "You'll be fine in the shade of the tree. I won't be gone long."

She exited the car, clutching her handbag to her side. She set her jaw tight with determination, straightened her shoulders and strode across the dirt.

The door opened before she even reached the porch.

"Mrs. Winter?"

"Hector?"

The small gray-haired man with the wire-rimmed

glasses nodded once. He had to be four inches shorter than her own five-ten. Her confidence rose.

He waved her into the foyer, closing the door behind her. "I was sorry to hear about your husband. He was a *generous* patron."

Pamela reached into her back pocket and pulled out a thick white envelope. "I can be just as generous. You have the papers?"

"Of course." He held a large flat brown envelope. "The money first."

She laid the payment on the entryway table. Hector picked up the envelope and thumbed through the bills.

"You follow directions better than your husband," he said, handing her the documents.

Pamela's chest tightened as her fingertips closed over the envelope. She struggled to keep her hands from shaking and opened the top, sliding the papers out.

Certificate of Adoption.

She glanced at the signatures. "Perfect," she said, then briefly glancing at the other official-looking paperwork. "And the original birth certificates?"

"Inaccessible through a bit of misdirection." Hector shrugged. "Easier than providing citizenship paperwork for your husband, but more expensive." He walked to the door and opened it. "Just know, Mrs. Winter, that we now have a pact. I expect you to honor it. I look forward to working with you again in the future."

Pamela slipped the documents into her handbag and grasped the butt of her husband's revolver. "I won't be needing your help again, Hector."

She yanked out the gun and pulled the trigger.

A bright red stain bloomed on Hector's shirt. His mouth dropped open. He fell to his knees.

He keeled over, lying perfectly still. Pamela knelt down

to make certain he was dead, then rose and stepped over the body.

Wait. She couldn't leave. The money.

She rolled him over and grabbed the envelope of cash. "Thanks, Hector."

Without a glance back she locked the door and walked to the car. The baby blinked, her lower lip poking out. Pamela could see the tantrum coming.

"You be good, little girl, because you belong to me now. I'm your new mother. Well, I will be as soon as the procedure is completed."

Pamela tossed her purse into the seat, slid into the vehicle and shifted into Drive. Her lips tilted up in satisfaction, humming a lullaby.

Ashes, ashes, we all fall down.

DANIEL STOOD IN the doorway, his gun pointed at Hondo's sister. Lucy let out a high-pitched squeal, and her eyes rolled back into her head. Before Daniel could catch her, Hondo's sister had dropped a set of blankets and a pillow on the ground, and keeled over at Daniel's feet.

He let out a curse, lowered his weapon and knelt beside the unconscious woman.

An echoing curse roared from the motel's office three doors down. Hondo raced out and stared at Lucy.

"What the hell did you do to my sister?" He glared at Daniel.

"I guess I scared her." Daniel slid his weapon into the back of his jeans. "I didn't expect anyone."

Hondo scooped the slight woman into his arms. "Well, you want any extra blankets, you're coming to me. I sure as hell ain't knocking on this door again." He narrowed his gaze at Daniel. "That's one strike, Adams. You don't get three chances in my establishment. One more, you're out."

With Lucy in his arms, he turned his back to them.

"It's my fault," Raven said softly. "Daniel's worried about someone trying to hurt me."

Hondo looked over his shoulder, taking in Raven's pale face. His expression softened. "I'll take that into account, but y'all need to know something about my sister. Her husband damaged her bad. She used to be the sharpest kid in her class at school. Scholarship outta here and all. After what the bastard did to her, her mind is like a little girl's. She just don't understand this world no more. I won't be having her hurt again. By anyone."

He walked away, and Daniel closed the door, locking and chaining it. Guilt had him sucking in a long, deep breath. That and being inside. He didn't like the way the walls pressed in close around him. He flicked the window lock and shoved the glass up.

A slight breeze filtered from outside, and he slowed his breathing down, one count at a time. Yes, calmer. Much better. But he could use a minute.

He faced Raven. "You said you wanted a shower. Now might be the best time."

"Oh, if I could get clean right now, I'd love you forever—" Her eyes widened. "I mean…I'd really like that."

A blush crept up her cheeks, and a sudden tension rose between them. "Well," he said in an attempt to lighten the mood. "If that's what you offer when I say you can take a shower, I can't wait to see what happens when I ask you about dinner."

Her cheeks went crimson, and she looked away from him.

Her transparent emotion seduced him as much as her words. After years of wondering whether each person he spoke to was playing a game, he'd erected walls that she obviously hadn't. Honesty could be sexier than he imagined—and far more worrisome to his equilibrium.

He drew her to her feet, then tilted her chin up with his finger. "Don't be embarrassed. We're in a strange situation. Best find the humor in it when we can. How about we both agree that what happens in Trouble stays in Trouble? When you get your memory back, neither one of us leaves with any regrets."

She laid her hand against his scarred cheek. "You're a kind man, Daniel Adams," she whispered.

"You don't even know me, honey, if you're saying that."

"I know enough."

How could he respond? She didn't understand. What would happen if the PTSD hit while he was sleeping tonight? What if his phantoms reappeared, and he lost himself? What if he couldn't tell where he was, and he hit Raven like he'd hit that poor orderly during his recovery? Daniel had nearly killed the man who'd come up behind him and awakened him without warning. He'd been dreaming of Bellevaux, and the guy had almost paid the ultimate price.

She stood, a bit unsteadily. Shoving the fears aside, he guided her to the bathroom with a hand at her back. He paused at the door. "Do you need help?"

"Thanks, but…I can manage." She wouldn't meet his gaze.

"Sure. That's good." He scuffed his boot on the rug, anything to take away the awareness that Raven was going to be in that room, totally naked, water sluicing down that amazing body. He'd have to take a shower after her. A cold one. "Go easy on your wound."

She touched the injury. "The doc told me what to do."

Raven passed him and started to shut the door.

"Don't lock it," he said.

"I won't."

"Call me if you need me."

"I won't," she said. "Need you, I mean."

Daniel shook his head. "Go get wet."

The door closed a little harder than necessary, and he laughed. Then Daniel grabbed a chair and sat down at the window, staring outside into the now-darkened sky.

The stars weren't as bright as they'd been when he had bedded down in the middle of nowhere, but Trouble, Texas, didn't have many lights to drown out the flickering flames in the sky. He let out a slow, deep breath and closed his eyes, counting backward from one hundred.

Images swirled in his mind. Memories. His heart raced.

With a slight prayer, he opened his eyes.

The past dissolved. The ceiling remained the old popcorn texture. No centuries-old stone blocks in front of his eyes.

"So far so good, mutt," he grumbled at Trouble. He'd just keep looking out that window.

The sound of the shower's spray filtered through the bathroom door.

Oh, crap. Naked. She was naked in there by now.

The dog hopped off the bed and settled next to the thin walnut-colored barrier, as if guarding her in case Daniel succumbed to his lascivious thoughts. "You've fallen for her, haven't you, boy? So could I, if I'm not careful."

The phone in his pocket vibrated. He glanced at the screen. A familiar name flashed—*Noah Bradford.* He hadn't seen that name since he'd taken off from Langley.

"I thought you were out saving the world."

Noah Bradford, the operative whose moniker, The Falcon, sent fear and frustration through most terrorist organizations in the Middle East, chuckled. "I should be, but it looks like I've gotta save your sorry ass instead. Our friends in Carder put out the word that you were in jail, possibly facing some impressive charges. Figured I'd come laugh at you before I bailed you out."

"As you can tell, I'm already out."

"Yeah, heard that, too. Would have been nice if I had heard it from you. Don't you ever answer your damn phone?"

"I've been…busy."

"I bet you have, but you've been incommunicado for months. You okay?"

Noah had been in on Daniel's rescue. Noah, more than most people, knew exactly the damage that had been done to Daniel's body and mind.

"I was ready to track you down, Daniel, and you know once I get on a trail, I don't give up until I get my man."

Daniel had been dangerous as an operative, but Noah was downright deadly. "I'm doing better," Daniel said, staring through the glass. And he was doing better.

"Must be, if you're at that fleabag motel and not in jail. You inside or outside?" Noah asked, before Daniel could call him on how Noah knew his exact location.

Then again, the man collected high-tech classified gadgets like most men collected baseball cards or porn magazines.

"I'm inside."

"Yeah?" The surprise in Noah's voice was telling.

"Got the window open, and I'm half hanging out of it, but I'm inside four walls and not freaking," Daniel admitted.

"Good job. There's hope for you yet."

"So what's with all this concern for me all of a sudden?"

"First off," Noah said, sounding a lot more serious, "I didn't think you'd fare all that well in jail. Second, Sheriff Blake Redmond filled in CTC about your problem."

"Blake is one damn talkative guy lately. Not sure I'm liking that."

"Tough. Friends watch out for friends, especially the ones too stubborn to ask for help themselves when they're up to their ass in alligators."

Daniel exhaled a frustrated breath. "So what did my good ex-buddy Blake tell you?"

"That you've got yourself a woman who was buried alive and no leads. That, while your butt was in jail, someone tried to take her out again. Ransom takes his job as CTC head honcho seriously. He's pissed you never called him, seeing as this is what CTC handles. He told me to pull out all the stops to help you. He wants you on the team bad, my friend. Help is on the way."

"Where are you now?" Daniel asked.

"Approaching a certain copper mine outside of town," Noah said. "Blake wanted to make the trip, but Deputy Smithson just returned to duty after being in a coma. I'm here to make sure the new CTC forensics guy, Elijah, doesn't piss off the Midland crime-scene team with his off-the-chart brain and irritating tenacity. He's good, and he knows it, and he's not shy about expressing his opinion. He's probably forgotten more about the science of dead bodies than these yahoos ever learned."

"Have you seen the location where she was left?" Daniel asked.

Noah let out a low curse. "Just pictures some deputy took. I gotta hand it to you for going in there. That place is a claustrophobic death trap. I went stir-crazy viewing the stills, and I hadn't been held…" His voice trailed off.

Held captive in a dungeon for months.

Daniel heard the words in his mind as if Noah had uttered them.

"I had to go in the mine. The dog wouldn't let up, and

when I heard someone alive in there, I didn't have much choice," Daniel said.

"I'm impressed, but going in there had to have been tough."

"Knowing someone is out there now, trying to kill Raven, is worse."

"I see…"

Noah's tone of voice definitely changed, and Daniel cursed, hating that he'd revealed even that much about his feelings for Raven. "There's nothing to see."

"Right. Well, just know that we're doing our best. Some local engineers are bringing equipment and supplies to stabilize the mine, so we can get a camera into the pocket where you found her. With luck, we can shore up everything long enough to retrieve the evidence," Noah said. "I'll let you know when we get in."

"Thanks, Noah." Daniel paused. "I… It means a lot—"

"Don't you go all touchy-feely on me. I got a reputation to uphold."

Daniel let out a chuckle. "Sorry. It's all that psychobabble the shrinks fed me at Langley."

"I'm glad it's helping," Noah stated. "And I'm really glad you're doing better."

Noah ended the call, and Daniel stilled. *Am I doing better? Am I ready to face the past...and the future?*

He stared at his phone and clicked on the voice mail button. A long list of messages came up. One message from Noah. A couple from his loquacious buddy, Sheriff Blake Redmond. A half dozen from Ransom, the head of CTC. And fifteen from his mom that seemed to jump up and slap him upside the head with his rotten-son status. She must be furious with him by this time.

A sharp curse escaped. Man, he didn't want to call her.

He'd pressed the first few buttons of her number when

someone appeared about ten feet outside the window in the unkempt side yard.

“Hey, you in there,” Hondo yelled. “Don’t shoot me. Your phone is off the hook, and I wasn’t about to knock on your door. I brought your friend some more cookies. They’re still hot.” [illegible]ead. Who was this guy? The Betty Crocker of Trouble, Texas, disguised as a Hell’s Angel? “Okay, I’ll unlock the door.”

Hondo held up a bag to the window. “These are for your friend ’cause I made her feel bad.” He scowled. “But none for you. It’s your fault I had to give Lucy a sedative.”

Daniel opened the door and took the bag. The smell of fresh-baked cookies filled the room. He groaned in appreciation and started to peer inside.

Hondo slapped Daniel’s hand. “I said no cookies for you. Especially not my chocolate-chip-oatmeal specials. Won the county fair blue ribbon last year.”

“I promise.”

Hondo paused. “Maybe you can have one after your lady eats her fill—since you seem to be taking care of her all right. She looks like she needs a lot of help. Those are some bad bruises around her throat, and I confirmed with Galloway that you didn’t put them there. He said you’re protecting her.”

Daniel glanced at the bathroom. “When she lets me.”

“Women can be ornery like that sometimes.” He looked around the hallway, then stepped closer. “If you need anything, I don’t just bake cookies.”

He lifted the pant leg of his jeans, and Daniel recognized the Bowie strapped to Hondo’s ankle. A look of understanding passed between the two men.

“Hopefully it won’t come to that, but it’s good to know.”

The big man slipped away, closing the door behind him,

and Daniel placed the white sack on the nightstand. He settled in the chair again, took a deep breath and dialed.

He braced himself for her anger, but if he was humble enough—

"Daniel Aaron Adams, why in tarnation didn't [illegible] me back for the past three months[illegible]

So much for a conciliatory greeting. He winced and held the phone away from his ear. "Hi, Mom. It's kind of a long story."

"I'm not going anywhere, so start talking. And remember, I can tell when you're lying."

THE MINE HADN'T changed except a few more piles of rocks had fallen from the ceiling. Not in the six years since Christopher's father had dragged him and Tad out of there during one very interesting spring break.

Tad's dad hadn't cared enough to punish them for messing around in the condemned caves, but Bill Winter had beaten Christopher enough for both fathers. The bruises had barely healed by the time school restarted. His mom had given him a note so he didn't have to undress during gym. No sense in inviting questions about the contusions decorating his back and legs.

Christopher twined the detonator wire on the dynamite and placed it near Christina's hand-carved box. He'd used his father's money to order online the best toy box ever for his adopted baby sister…and fill it with everything his dad had taken away from him over the years. What a waste, but it couldn't be helped.

He did a final check on his setup and handed the detonator cord to Tad. Back in the day they had used blasting caps they'd found in the old sheds near the mines. It's a wonder they hadn't blown themselves up. They were more sophisticated now.

"We're covering for your mom, dude?" Tad said, wrapping the explosives. He cut the cord, then wiped his hands on his jeans. "This is too twisted. I thought it was your old man who was one beer short of a six-pack." He rose from his charge and looked at the carpet. "She really did a number on that lady. With that much blood, I'm surprised she didn't die."

"Quit complaining. You wouldn't get to hunt if she were a corpse."

"Too true." Then Tad turned. "Shh." He stilled, listening intently. "Did you hear something?"

Christopher paused. "Sounds like a truck engine." He cursed, running around the bend to the mine's entrance. He peered into the light. The diesel engine of a huge flatbed loaded down with a small bulldozer rumbled down the road toward them. Smoke puffed in the air.

"Quick!" he shouted. "Hide the explosives."

Tad camouflaged his, and Christopher quickly concealed the dynamite behind the toy box and grabbed his hunting rifle. "Let's get out of here."

Tad at his heels with the detonator, Christopher raced toward daylight. The truck rumbled to a halt not too far from the mine's entrance. The driver jumped out. Dust spewed into the air as a sheriff's car pulled up beside the equipment.

Christopher shrank into the shadows. "Watch for an opening. We can't be seen."

An SUV pulled up, and the deputy turned his back on them.

"Now," Christopher hissed. He grabbed the detonator. Not looking around to see if Tad followed, Christopher sprinted to an outcropping of rocks and dove behind the cover.

Seconds later Tad slid behind him. “Leave me behind next time, why don’t you?” he bit out.

“I knew you’d make it,” Christopher lied. Belly first, he crawled between two mounds of rocks. A sharp stone scraped his belly, but he ignored the pain. They had to get far enough away to avoid the blast.

The desert offered more camouflage than he remembered. Christopher hunkered down behind a berm and peeked around a mesquite bush. A crime-scene van pulled up and two men filed into the cave, followed by a guy sporting a large case.

Then a deadly looking man exited an SUV. He pulled the deputy aside. Their conversation turned heated.

“I don’t care what the forensics team wants. Sheriff Galloway gave us the leeway, so I’m ordering you *not* to remove any evidence from the crime scene. At least not until they get here.”

Christopher couldn’t make out the deputy’s whine.

“Just do it,” the man said. “If we’re going to save Jane Doe’s life, she needs to remember, and this cave is the only thing familiar to her. It needs to stay intact.” He glanced at his watch. “They’ll be here soon. If anything gets pulled out of that mine, you won’t just have the sheriff to worry about.”

Tad’s eyes went wide. “Did I just hear what I think I heard?”

Christopher smiled. “I’m living right these days.”

“The timing has to be perfect.” Tad fingered the detonator. “But it was your dad’s mine. They could tie it back to you.”

“My father sold it years ago for a mountain of cash, most of it mine now,” Christopher argued, setting the detonator to his side. A scorpion skittered across the sand.

Christopher slid his blade from its sheath and let the knife fly. He stabbed the creature in two without a breath.

"Must be nice to be rich," Tad said. "A dishonorable discharge doesn't do the bank account any good."

"Yeah, well, I'll pay you for the help. I deserve that money. At least a dollar a punch," Christopher said. "We just gotta wait until our target arrives. She'll go into that mine to figure out what happened to her, but it won't matter what she remembers. She won't be coming out."

DANIEL GRIPPED THE phone at his mom's stubborn words. She wouldn't let him hang up. He squeezed the guilt of not calling before now into submission. The motel room's air turned thin, and he sucked in a slow, deep breath. He leaned forward, huddling protectively over the phone as if his mom would be able to sense his desire to hug her. "I'm sorry I just disappeared like that."

A choked sob filtered through the phone. "God, I've been so worried. Are you okay?"

His throat closed off a bit. "Sure."

She didn't say a word. He closed his eyes for a moment and bit his lip.

"I told you not to lie to me, Daniel."

He shook his head. Damn the woman; she caught him every time. He'd never been able to deceive Jeanette Adams. Not as a kid. And obviously not as an adult. Even through the phone.

"How are you, son? Really?"

"Honestly?" He swallowed past the lump building in his throat. This was why he hadn't called her. He loved his family, and he knew they loved him, but his emotions had become like live grenades waiting for the pin to pull. One wrong touch could be deadly. He couldn't protect himself, or her, from feelings that were too unpredictable. "I don't know."

"The dreams still giving you trouble?" she asked, her voice concerned, her sorrow seeping through.

Daniel closed his eyes, flashing on the nightmares, when the darkness had shredded his soul. She'd witnessed every horrifying moment of those first two weeks. She'd seen him shut down, responding to nothing and no one. She'd stroked his hair and whispered comforting words like she had when he was ten, and he'd broken his arm sliding into third base.

She'd seen him stare at the room and not see the hospital, but the dungeon walls of Bellevaux.

She'd held him when he'd cried out in pain during the night, in a despair so raw he'd possessed no control. She'd hurt for him when the orderlies restrained him to the bed while he screamed and swore like a crazy man. She'd pitied him, and he'd hated it, but that wasn't the worst of it.

The lowest moment he could remember was one horrible day. He'd thought he was better. The therapy session had gone well. He'd come back to his room, and she'd stood there, waiting for him, her hand adjusting the blinds with the cord.

A lousy cord.

The twined string had morphed into a leather whip. He'd lunged at her, death in his heart. She'd let out a small cry, and he'd come back to reality, but he'd seen her eyes, the second he'd recognized the fear on her face. Not *for* him. Fear *of* him.

He'd seen that same expression when she'd looked at his dad.

Something inside him had died in that moment.

The sound of the shower ceased. Daniel stiffened, but Raven didn't come out. He wanted to hang up and knock on the bathroom door to check on her, but she needed her time.

And he needed to make his mother understand.

"Mom," he said slowly, "I'm like Dad. I know it, and so do you." He couldn't live with destroying his family any more than his father had. He had to protect them, even if that meant hurting them—and himself.

Silence echoed through the receiver. He could barely make out a few shuddering breaths.

"The dungeon still comes back, Mom. I see it, where it's not. And the sounds. The screams. I live through that time every night. Even during the day. Just like Dad."

"But do you believe what you see is real?" she asked, her voice trembling with the question. "Do you think you're actually there?"

"It feels real," he said. "The stench. The pain." He rubbed his wrist. "I still wake up screaming, as if the whip is cutting into my back."

She bit back a small sob. "God, son, I want to kill the man who hurt you all over again, but that's a nightmare. You can't control it." She paused, and Daniel gripped the phone even tighter.

"Daniel, when you're awake—when an episode hits—do you believe you are in that dungeon in Bellevaux?"

He rubbed the scar on his cheek, then thrust his fingers through his hair. "Sometimes. Sometimes I have to fight really hard to remember, but mostly I have a double sense, and I can figure out where I am."

He heard a soft sigh. "I talked to your doctor," she said. "PTSD has a spectrum. You're not where your father was. Aaron couldn't tell the difference between the past and present. Ever. He was lost. You're not."

Daniel gripped the windowsill hard and breathed in the

cool evening air. He wanted to believe her. "Dad was okay sometimes," he whispered. "I remember."

"I know," she said. "Those days gave me hope, but they never lasted. Even years later, your father still couldn't find his way out of that mental hell. He couldn't bring himself back to reality. You can. That means you can regain your life."

"But—"

"You are *not* like your father. At all. You already have a control he never did." Her voice took on an edge he hadn't heard since one of his sisters hadn't come home by curfew one night. "Believe me. You are my son, and I will fight you for your survival."

Unable to keep still, Daniel rose, then paced back and forth, his mind whirling.

"Honey, come home. Try it. Your sister's getting married soon. It would mean the world to her for you to be there."

"I still don't trust myself." Daniel rubbed the base of his neck. "All those cars backfiring. Construction clanging like those damn metal bars closing. A crowd of people jammed into one room. Champagne corks popping. Nowhere to escape. I could snap just like he did. I won't ruin the wedding. Or their lives."

"They need you here. They trust you. So do I."

"You can't know I'll be okay," Daniel said. "You always said Dad would get better, but he never did. You told us he'd be fine, and he'd find peace, but he found it at the end of a gun."

The phone line went quiet. Too quiet. Daniel winced in regret. "I'm sorry. I didn't mean that."

"Yes, you did, and you're right. I let hope cloud my words and thoughts, seeing healing where there wasn't any. I wanted you and your sisters to still love him, to remember the man he used to be. I didn't understand just how deep his demons went."

"You don't know how deep mine go, either. I'm not the man I once was. Until I know for sure that I can keep it together, I'm not coming home. I love you and the girls. I don't want to let them down, but they've been through enough. I'd rather they hate me for what I didn't do than for what I did."

"I learned the hard way not to hide from this illness, Daniel. If I believed you were a danger to yourself or them, I'd snap you into the hospital faster than you could reach for your weapon." She paused. "Trust me."

"I do. It's trusting myself that's the problem. Bye." He ended the call and pressed the phone against his forehead.

I miss you.

Chapter Six

Raven stood frozen in place in the bathroom, holding on to the door she'd just opened, staring at Daniel. Shock still reverberated through her. Daniel had a home somewhere. A woman and girls who wanted him back.

She wanted to be hurt…or angry…or something. She'd come to think of him as hers. Her savior, her protector… just hers. All of a sudden, the outside world had blown apart the small bubble of safety she'd discovered in his presence.

She'd been attacked, her memory lost, but that didn't excuse not seeing his turmoil or his pain. How selfish could she be? She didn't want to be that kind of person, but she was scared. Her belly rolled at the thought of being alone—without the one man she could trust. She needed him. But not at this cost.

Her fingers bit into the wooden door so hard that they cramped. She couldn't take her gaze off him. His entire body sagged in despair.

Her feelings didn't matter. Seeing how broken Daniel looked right now pushed her own needs aside. She wanted to comfort him, but he straightened his shoulders. His face went expressionless as stone as he shook off his emotions.

Doubting he would welcome her witnessing him so vulnerable, she cleared her throat and shoved the door so it thudded against the wall, pretending she was just coming out of the bathroom.

His narrowed gaze snapped to hers. He hesitated for a moment, then rose and crossed the room, picking up a white paper bag on the way. "Hondo says hi."

She took the sack from him and studied his features, searching for some chink in his armor.

"What?" he demanded.

She didn't know if she'd been brave when she knew her own name, but his intensity didn't encourage questions. Would she normally have backed off? She had no idea, and she had to know.

"You're leaving, aren't you?" she said. "I don't blame you. I'm more trouble than you asked for. I understand."

He pocketed the phone and glared at her. "I told you. I'm not going anywhere. Not until you're safe. We may not know each other very well, but I keep my promises."

"Your wife—"

Understanding lit his eyes, and they crinkled at the corners when he gave her a slight grin. "I'm not married, Raven. That was my mom."

"Oh." The wave of relief that swept through Raven nearly buckled her knees. It wasn't right, though. She had no business feeling this way. She didn't even know him.

He sidled up to her. "How much did you hear?"

She couldn't meet his gaze, and his proximity sent a shiver up her spine. "I didn't mean to eavesdrop. And it was just the last few sentences. Something about not going home and loving the girls. I thought you might have kids."

"I was talking about my sisters."

"That's great. I mean, it must be nice to have siblings." She groaned, sinking onto the bed, burying her head in her hands. "Just hog-tie me and shut me up before I make an even bigger fool of myself."

He tilted her chin up. “I’m flattered,” he said, his smile gentle. “Now, dig into the sack, and you’ll find enough chocolate to distract you.”

“Why would that help?”

“According to my sisters, it’s a universal girl thing.” He shrugged.

“I don’t remember, but I’ll take a chance.” She opened the bag, and a sweet smell wafted from inside. She inhaled and her stomach grumbled. Chocolate chip. She lifted out one warm cookie, took a bite and closed her eyes, moaning in pleasure. “I think we have a winner. This is amazing.” She pinched off a small bite, holding it to his lips. “Try it.”

“Hondo has rules…”

“Then we won’t tell him,” she whispered. “But this cookie is orgasmic.”

At the words, her shocked gaze captured his equally stunned one.

His eyes darkened, and Raven’s breath stuttered. “I mean, it’s really, really good.”

“Then I’ll definitely have some.” His tone deepened, he leaned forward and snagged the morsel from her fingertips, licking off a small bit of chocolate that clung to her skin.

She cleared her throat. “Best thing you ever tasted. Right?”

With a run of his tongue across his lips, he stared at her. “Yeah, and the cookie’s not half-bad, either.”

She bit her lower lip. “I want to—” Before her brain stopped her, she pressed her lips to his mouth, and her body leaned into him.

Daniel didn’t resist. His arm snaked around her waist and tightened his hold, drawing her to him. He took over, parting her lips, exploring her mouth, holding her captive with his caress.

Lord, he could kiss.

Forget chocolate. She had a whole new favorite taste. Raven wrapped her arms around his neck and held him closer, taking the kiss even deeper.

The room faded away until all she knew was his touch, his scent, his passion. She nipped at his lower lip, wanting even more, rocking against the hardness pressing into her belly.

With a growl he eased back. "This is a bad idea," he said softly.

"I don't care," she whispered against his mouth. And she didn't. She just wanted to feel. This crazy heat that was going through her was something she wanted to know more about. She couldn't believe she'd ever felt anything like what Daniel made her feel.

Surely I'd remember something like this.

Ignoring his intended retreat, she held his face in her hands and kissed him again, reveling in the lightning that sparked from her core, up through her breasts. She pushed them against his chest to ease the ache.

"Wow. Where has this feeling been all my life? I like it!" She couldn't stop the words and bit her lip. "The doctor said frontal lobe injuries often reduce inhibitions a bit. Is this what he meant?"

A small growl escaped from deep inside Daniel's chest. "I don't know."

"Well, I certainly hope so." She clutched at his shirt and tugged him closer.

Suddenly his phone vibrated on the table with an insistent hum. Daniel let out a long, slow breath. "I hate phones."

He clicked Talk and dragged it to his ear. "Adams." His voice came out husky.

Raven leaned in to listen.

"You two okay?" Sheriff Galloway asked. "You sound funny."

"We're fine." Daniel put his arm around Raven. "We're holed up in the motel. By the way, thanks for paying for a week in advance."

"I didn't figure you carried much cash, and Raven doesn't seem like she's going to be remembering her bank accounts anytime soon," Galloway said. "But on the good news front, preliminary blood tests on the denim material that your dog tore show it's a potential match for Raven's attacker. Type AB negative kind of narrows things down with this small-town population."

"Trouble knows whose it is. He'll recognize the guy if he comes across the scent again," Daniel said.

Trouble's ears perked up at the mention of his name, and he cocked his head. Raven petted the sweetie, and he leaned up against her leg. She caressed behind his ears and smiled as he pushed his head harder against her hand.

"What about samples from the mine? Can they retrieve them?" Daniel shook his head at Trouble, and Raven simply smiled.

"Your CTC colleagues indicated the engineering crew believes they can stabilize the mine long enough to process the crime scene. If nothing else goes wrong out there, they can be done by the end of the day."

"They haven't moved anything yet, have they?" Daniel asked.

"They're on hold until you get there," the sheriff said.

"We'll leave soon," Daniel said and ended the call.

Go back to the mine? Raven's stomach rolled at the thought. "I don't know—"

"The doctor said you should retrace your steps. See if anything out there triggers a memory now that your symptoms are improving."

Despite her fear, she nodded. “We’re not going to find out the truth sitting in this motel room, are we?”

Daniel gave her an approving nod. “Exactly. And you’ll be protected. I’ll be there, and so will the deputy and two men from CTC.” At her questioning glance, he shrugged. “I have a few friends with some skills that could come in handy.”

Men like him. Raven didn’t have to ask more. She clasped her heart-shaped locket. “I have a baby out there, and I need to find her. No matter what the danger.”

He crossed the room and took out his gun. A click sounded, and the magazine fell into his hand. He checked it and then reloaded. “We’re going to find out what happened to the baby. I promise you that.”

Raven went still. Daniel hadn’t said he would *find* the baby. Only that he’d discover what happened. Did he think her baby was dead?

For all her earlier bravery, Raven could not get up the courage to ask him.

THE ROAD TO the mine looked different from a truck. Daniel glanced at Raven. The afternoon sun hit the side of her face. Bruises had started rising near her temple—green, blue and yellow mottled in a painful-looking pattern. She’d been through so much.

She clutched the locket. “How much farther?”

He slowed the truck to a crawl, and Trouble let out a bark from the bed of the pickup. Daniel studied her expression, searching for any sign of recognition. “Anything look familiar?”

“I don’t know. Dirt road, desert, shrubs, mountains in the distance.” The intensity on her face didn’t waver as she gazed out the front windshield at the curving road heading toward the mine where Daniel and Trouble had found her. But with each mile, he watched the light fade from her gaze. Her hand tightened on his, and his gut twisted. His shoulders tensed. Without Raven's memory, everyone they came into contact with was a suspect.

They came within a mile of the mine, and her chin fell to her chest. "This is useless. I don't recognize anything."

"This is the first try, darlin'. You still have healing to do. Cut yourself some slack."

She glanced over at him. "We both know this is the only lead. Don't patronize me. I may not have a memory, but I'm not a fool."

"Sorry," he said. "You're right. But wishing won't make it happen. There's forensic evidence in that cave, including blood. We have a lot of trails to follow."

Raven twisted in her seat. "DNA from the blood should help," she mused. "Comparing the thirteen core loci could get a match using CODIS."

Her eyes widened as he stared at her.

"Oh, wow, where did that come from?" She fell back into the seat.

"Well, Ms. Scientist. What else do you know about DNA profiling?"

He could almost see her mind whirl with effort.

"I know a lot. A whole lot." Excitement lit her face. "Did you know that if you have a CODIS profile or even a small sample of DNA, you can falsify the evidence? But you can also test for fake DNA."

She went on to describe in detail exactly what that entailed, but the explanation went way over Daniel's head.

"So you're a lab rat," he said. "That's pretty complex stuff to remember. You could give Elijah a run for his money."

"I don't know about that, but I think I was a scientist of some sort. That will help, right?"

"If you're from around here, we can narrow the search to biotech companies, universities and the like. Ask if they're missing a beautiful, brilliant brain," Daniel said.

She smiled at him, hope returning to her eyes. He'd wanted to see her smile again, to wipe away the hurt any way he could. More and more, he understood why his mother had kept the truth of his father's illness from them when they were kids. Hope meant everything.

The truck rounded the final curve leading to the mine. Several vehicles created a makeshift lot just east of the entrance to the mine.

Daniel pulled in near them, parked and turned in his seat. "Okay, let's take this slow. Focus on all your senses—sounds, smells, the feel of the earth beneath your feet. Memories are tied to those other senses even more than sight."

He knew that firsthand.

He exited the vehicle and scanned the cleared area in front of the mine for anything out of place. With a quick look toward the desert with its small hills and occasional shrub, he opened the door for her, as satisfied as he could be.

She slid out, and Trouble jumped from the back of the truck, standing guard beside her. Daniel motioned for her to stay put as he walked away, with her always in his sight.

Galloway's full-time deputy walked over and tipped his hat. "Deputy Adams, sir."

Daniel grimaced. Trouble's tail stiffened. His ears went flat, and a warning growl rumbled from him.

The deputy paused. "He bite?"

"Not usually, but he seems to hate uniforms. I wouldn't push it."

The kid backed off.

Noah Bradford walked up to Daniel and crooked a brow. "Did I hear him say 'deputy'?"

"It's temporary."

"CTC will be glad to hear that."

Daniel hadn't seen his friend for months. Noah now had a close-trimmed beard, which meant he was probably headed on a mission soon. Daniel liked to change up his appearance. Disguises had saved his life more than once.

Daniel held out his hand. "I'm glad you're here. What's going on?"

Noah swiped at the dust on his shirt. "The engineers shored up the entrance, but the place is a death trap. We were waiting for you."

"Thanks," Daniel said.

Noah glanced at the deputy. "Go keep an eye on Elijah, deputy. He might steal some of your evidence."

The deputy's face paled. "He wouldn't!" The kid took off back to the edge of the mine, where a tall man knelt next to several cases of equipment.

"That CTC's infamous new forensics lead?" Daniel asked, grinning at the deputy's nervousness. Elijah's ornery reputation had become legendary in a matter of months.

Noah smiled. "Yeah. Guy's a pit bull when it comes to evidence. Not much of a talker, though."

"And you are?"

"Compared to Elijah, yeah. I'm all about communication." Noah's sharp gaze took in Daniel's appearance. "You look better than you did on our last foray in Carder. Guess the two-thousand-mile trek did you some good."

"Maybe." Daniel looked over his shoulder at Raven, who stood off to the side staring intently at the mine. She closed her eyes for a moment, her brow furrowed.

"I read the report. You got her out of that cave, Daniel.

I'd have put up a few grand against those odds last time I saw you. Hell, your heart pounded like a rabbit's when you were sitting in a cockpit, and the damn thing had a window."

"She needed help." Daniel studied her black hair shining in the sunlight and the bruise on her temple. "She's got guts, Noah. She could have wrapped up in a ball and imploded, but she just doesn't quit."

"You like her."

Daniel rubbed the base of his neck. "Yeah. I shouldn't. What if--?"

Noah crossed his arms. "The man in front of me won't let her down." He paused. "I wasn't sure when I should give you this, but…I think now's the time." Noah turned to an SUV parked a few feet away. He opened the back door and revealed a small bag. Without words he reached in and pulled out a leather whip.

Daniel froze. Brown leather, braided, a brass seal around the handle. He recognized it well. The crest of the Duke of Sarbonne from Bellevaux. He couldn't take his eyes off the torture weapon. His palms went sweaty. A crack sounded in his memory. His gaze snapped to Noah's. "What the hell are you playing at?"

"Tough love, my brother." Noah shoved it at Daniel. "I brought it back from Bellevaux. I didn't know if I'd ever give it to you. The shrink said to use my own judgment." Noah glanced at Raven. "I think you're ready to break the hold the memories of this whip have over you."

Daniel shoved the whip at Noah. "Get rid of it. Bury it, burn it, trash it. Just get it the hell away from me."

"Conquer your demons." Noah gripped Daniel's arm and forced Daniel's hand around the whip.

With some sort of twisted need, Daniel let him and didn't throw him to the ground.

Noah clasped Daniel's shoulder. "The bastard who used this on you is dead, but he still lives in your head. Crack it until the sound doesn't haunt you any longer. Until you break its hold, Sarbonne wins. He stole so much from you, Daniel. Don't let him have your soul."

The leather felt stiff in Daniel's hand. His heart pounded; his gut bubbled with a fury unlike anything he'd ever known. His jaw throbbed until it ached. "Sometimes you can't win," he gritted. "My dad didn't."

"But you can. We've both seen the men who come home with more demons than they can live with. Some move on. Some don't. Go forward, Daniel. For yourself. And for her." Noah nodded over at Raven who'd turned to stare at them, her face concerned. She took a step toward them.

Daniel jerked the hand holding the whip behind his back. He wasn't ready for her questions. "Fine. I'll take it. But the first chance I get, I'm tossing it out the window. I want to forget."

"And that's worked so well for you, Forrest Gump."

Daniel bit out a four-letter word.

Noah's expression turned serious. "Look, do what you want with it, Daniel, however you can exorcise the demons. It's in your hands now." With that, Noah turned and headed toward Elijah.

Daniel crossed to the truck and tossed the whip into the back.

"Who was that?" Raven asked.

"Someone with a warped idea of friendship." Daniel frowned.

Raven touched his arm. "Are you okay?"

He turned to her. "I'll be fine," he lied, unwilling to reveal how much seeing that damn weapon nearly sent him to his knees. "How about you? Any more memories?"

"You," she said softly. "All I remember is you."

A rifle shot echoed through the air. Daniel shoved Raven into the ground next to the truck, then pushed her beneath the vehicle. In one swift movement he'd placed his body between her and the gunfire, and pulled out his weapon.

A bullet ricocheted off the metal just over their heads. "It's coming from behind that dirt ledge!" Noah shouted, pulling out his own weapon. "Everyone take cover in the mine."

Men ran from their positions, preparing to go into the cave. Several shots followed them in.

Almost simultaneously a thwack hit the ground near Daniel. "Two shooters!" Daniel shouted. No time for waiting. They were too vulnerable out here. "Cover us."

Elijah and Noah fired at the mound of dirt hiding the gunmen. Daniel grabbed Raven's hand. "Run!"

In seconds they dove into the cave. Elijah followed. He met Daniel's gaze with a hard look. "This the idiot who came after Raven before?"

Daniel had expected Elijah to be a science geek, but this man could hold his own in a battle. Huge, brilliant—and pissed.

Daniel nodded.

"Noah's positioned outside behind the rock outcropping, but he doesn't have an endless supply of bullets," Elijah said.

"What do you have for firearms?" Daniel asked. "No way we can stay in here."

Elijah nodded in agreement. "But it's almost like the shooter drove us in…or he's a horrible shot."

"I don't like this." Daniel grabbed the small flashlight still hooked to his belt.

"If he wants us in here," Elijah said, "there's got to be a good reason."

"Yeah. Or a damned bad one."

"Anyone with a flashlight, look around quickly for anything out of place."

Within minutes, a shout came out. "I found something."

Daniel raced around the bend.

Elijah pointed at the hint of red primer cord nearly concealed beneath a pile of rocks.

"It's rigged to blow," Daniel cursed. "Deputy, get everyone out. Cover them."

Elijah walked the area, then cursed. "There's another one." He pulled gloves from his pocket, snapped them on and pulled out a knife, taking it to the bloodstained carpet.

"No time for that," Daniel said. "Hurry."

He raced around the bend. "Everybody head east toward the rocks," Daniel shouted. "Don't stop until you reach safety. We'll try to cover you."

"Noah, we've got to come out!" Daniel yelled. "Lay down some cover."

A spray of bullets erupted from Noah's hiding place.

"Go! Now!"

The men hurled out of the opening just as Elijah skidded beside Daniel holding two evidence bags: one with a piece of carpet, the other with what looked to be wood shavings covered in blood.

Daniel glared at him.

"It's our one chance," Elijah said. "You know it as well as I do."

Daniel grabbed Raven's hand and bolted, his gun blazing. "Stay behind me."

Terror lined her face, but she ran. Bullets smacked the rocks above them. Daniel leaped behind a boulder and tugged Raven with him.

A fireball burst from the mouth of the mine, a conflagration shooting through the air. Heat seared the air around

Daniel and Raven, but the boulder blocked the worst of it. Nearby, two vehicles were engulfed in flames.

The second bomb exploded, and the ground beneath them shuddered. Daniel wrapped his arms around Raven's head and ducked down, shielding her. A rain of dirt pummeled them.

When the earth had settled, Daniel took a quick glance at the cave. The entire mouth of the mine was packed with dirt and rubble.

An engine revved. They both turned to see Noah and Elijah standing in the dirt firing at an escaping van. Where had that come from? The vehicle must have been hidden behind one of the large berms off to the side of the road leading up to the mine.

"Damn it, they got away," Daniel said.

She raised her gaze to his. "What's so important about me and my baby that they want me dead, and were willing to kill all these innocent people to make it happen?"

Daniel couldn't hold back the fury building in his gut. "I don't know, but we're going to find out."

RAVEN SAT IN Daniel's truck, gripping the armrest with a death hold, her fingers numb. The entire scene had been surreal. Noah and Elijah had declared the area clear. They'd discovered dozens of spent casings from what they'd called a semiautomatic varmint rifle, two sets of footprints and skidding tire marks, but the snipers had vanished.

Several trucks and a lot of equipment had been burned. The place looked like a war zone. For a few minutes most of the crime-scene investigators had been shell-shocked, then the anger had hit, and they started collecting evidence—what little there was. The mine was blocked off. Permanently this time. The whole infrastructure had collapsed.

Noah and Elijah had stayed to help, but Daniel had wanted her out of there.

Raven slid a sidelong glance at him. Once again he'd saved her life. The muscle in his jaw throbbed with fury. His knuckles had whitened with his tense grip on the steering wheel. He kept checking the rearview mirror and the side mirrors.

Even Trouble stayed at attention, as if on guard. The dog had nine lives. He'd been in the truck when the nearby vehicles had gone up in flames. The mutt had been shaken, but he'd come out of the attack none the worse for wear.

"Are we going back to the motel?" Raven asked.

"For the moment. I don't like it. Someone was waiting for us at that damn mine. I shouldn't have taken you there until they were caught. I should have at least had a chopper clear the area," Daniel said. "I'm off my game. I put you in danger." He swerved to the side of the road and shoved the vehicle into Park. "I've been thinking about this for a while, Raven. I might not be the best person to help you. Noah can protect you in ways I can't. I'd like for you to go with him."

"No. I don't know him." She grabbed his arm. "I know you. I trust you. You protected me."

"You don't understand." He let out a slow stream of air. "I was held captive in Bellevaux last November and December. I was tortured, beaten, whipped and starved. They shattered my leg in three places. My ribs and hands weren't much better. I'm put together with bolts and screws. They messed with my head. I've got claustrophobia and PTSD. I get flashbacks. If something happened to you because I didn't know where I was…I couldn't live with that, Raven."

He looked away, his face devoid of expression, and she knew under normal circumstances he would never have revealed the truth, but it explained so much. Their time in the cave, how he could calm her down. He understood the panic, the fear. She couldn't think of anyone better to help her.

She slid closer to him, and his entire body stiffened. "I see you fighting your demons," she said softly. "Help me battle mine. I *have* to remember, Daniel, and I'm not sure I can do this alone. I trust you to help me."

Daniel shoved his hand through his hair. "You're making a mistake."

She crossed her arms in front of her chest. "I don't think so."

He pulled back onto the deserted highway. No matter what Raven said, he'd contact Noah. He didn't trust himself. Just as they entered Trouble's city limits, Daniel's phone rang.

He punched Speaker. "Adams."

A crackling voice filled the cab. "Elijah's equipment is toast. He can't test the evidence he salvaged. I have to fly him back to Carder. Do you want another CTC crew?"

Daniel rubbed his face. "I'll let you know. Keep me posted on the results." He paused. "The data probably won't hold up in court due to the chain of evidence issues, but that doesn't matter. Run Raven's prints and DNA through every database we've got. Local, federal, international. We *have* to identify her. We have to find her child and the baby's father," Daniel ordered.

"We'll do everything we can," Noah promised. "If you decide to come back with us, call within the hour. Otherwise, I'll keep in touch. And, Daniel, think about working with what I gave you. What have you got to lose?"

Raven shuddered. She had seen Noah hand off the whip to Daniel, had watched his automatic response. She hoped Daniel threw the whip away. Horrible thing.

"Got it." Daniel ended the call and turned to her. "We

should go with them. The company headquarters in Carder is a fortress. CTC can protect you."

Raven squeezed the locket in her hand. "Whoever wants me dead probably has my daughter, don't they?"

"It's a safe bet."

He didn't offer any comfort. How could he? Raven closed her eyes, knowing what she had to do. "The men who attacked us are my only connection to my child. I won't hide away somewhere protected while she could be..." Her voice broke. "I have to stay close. I have to try everything I can to remember. Maybe, if I set myself up as bait, I could get close enough to see one of their faces—"

"No way."

"What choice do we have? We have no solid leads. I have this locket. There was a toy box in that mine. Everything points to my baby being at the center of this crazy conspiracy. I'm not leaving town until I know." She looked up at him. "Please."

Daniel kneaded the back of his neck. "Noah gave me a computer program that thc CTC psychologist has been using to help witnesses and trauma victims remember details. If you want—"

She leaned forward, eagerness pulsing through her. "You don't even have to ask. What are we waiting for?"

Finally something to help her remember.

"Don't get your hopes up. It's experimental. It doesn't always work, and you're still physically bruised. We haven't tried this with anyone this recently injured. The concussion may affect it."

"It doesn't matter. We have to try. *I* have to try."

Daniel nodded cautiously, but for the first time since she had woken, Raven sensed possibilities.

"We need quiet, solitude, safety," he said. "The motel won't do. I'll need to find another location."

He pulled into the motel's parking lot in front of their room.

"We aren't safe here?"

"You're not safe anywhere. It's a small town. They know we're nearby. It's time to go off the grid."

Daniel exited the truck, then took her by the hand. She followed him, watching him as he walked to the front of the motel, looking around, his entire body alert. This was the warrior. This was the man who made her feel like she could breathe again.

The motel's office door opened up. Daniel's hand went to his midback, where she knew he tucked his weapon. Lucy stuck her head around the side.

Raven touched Daniel's arm. "Don't scare Lucy," she whispered.

He sent Lucy a slight nod and smiled at the timid woman. "What can we do for you?"

"Hondo made a batch of peanut butter cookies," she said quietly. "Can I bring them over without you shooting me up?"

"I don't—"

Raven shoved her elbow into Daniel's side. "Sure, Lucy. We'd love some."

"I don't like peanut butter," he muttered to Raven with a frustrated glare. "But I was going to say that I don't want her to be afraid of me."

"After scaring the woman to death, peanut butter is your new favorite food," Raven said. She brightened her smile. "I can't wait to try them, Lucy."

The woman grinned and walked toward them, carrying a small wicker basket. Hondo walked protectively behind her, glowering at Daniel, as all four made their way to room six.

"I don't think this was Hondo's idea," Daniel whispered to Raven, as he pushed his key into the lock and shoved open the door. "Go into the room and stay out of sight," he said. "No lights and don't go near the windows. I don't want to attract attention. Once they leave, we'll throw our stuff in the truck and get out of here."

Raven nodded. "Agreed."

She walked in and sat across the room, away from the door, while Lucy set her basket on the small table by the motel room window. Daniel hovered in an awkward attempt to help her, but Hondo walked in with a second basket and shoved him aside. With a sigh, Daniel lowered the blinds, dimming the available light, but blocking the view from outside.

Raven covered her mouth with a smile.

"These cookies are *not* my idea," Hondo said. "Lucy felt bad she fainted."

"I'm sorry I scared you," Daniel said, leaning against the wall next to Raven. She could tell he wanted to get this over with and pack.

Lucy poured milk into two glasses and laid out a spread of cookies and fruit. She even added a small vase of flowers before stepping back and admiring her handiwork.

"It's beautiful, Lucy," Raven said. "Thank you."

Lucy glared at Hondo. "See. Told you they'd like them," she said, wrinkling her nose. "But it's so dark in here. At least turn on the light—"

"No!" Daniel shouted as Lucy's form was thrown into silhouette against the blind.

The next moment, a spray of gunfire shattered the glass. Lucy fell to the ground. Hondo leaped toward his sister, and another volley of bullets peppered the motel room.

Daniel vaulted to the door, racing into the parking lot in time to see a car screech away.

Raven grabbed a towel and dropped to her knees beside Lucy. "Oh, my God, Lucy. Daniel, call 9-1-1."

Her heart twisted with guilt as she pressed at the wounds on Lucy's chest, trying to stop the flow of blood, but it seeped through. So much blood. Too much blood.

Daniel slammed back into the room, Trouble on his heels, and her gaze snapped to him. He plastered the phone at his ear. "We need an ambulance at Copper Mine Motel. Drive-by shooting. Two down. The car was a late model white sedan. The license plate was covered in mud, but my guess is Texas plates."

"Daniel," Raven choked, the towel turning red in her hands. "I need more."

He sprinted to the bathroom and threw her a set. She grabbed one and replaced the one that had soaked through. Trouble whimpered and lay in the corner while Daniel ran to Hondo. The big man let out a low moan. Daniel pressed a cloth against Hondo's bleeding shoulder and met Raven's gaze.

Her eyes burned with emotion when she looked down at Lucy's innocent face. "You're going to be okay. The ambulance is coming."

God, please let her be okay.

"Hondo," Lucy whispered. "I'm all bloody. Am I dying?"

Her brother shoved at Daniel, groaned and rolled toward her.

"No, baby girl," he said, his voice choked. "I promised Mom I'd take care of you. And I always keep my promises. You're going to be fine."

"It hurts," she whimpered. "I don't like it." Her voice trailed off, and her eyes closed.

Hondo struggled to his hands and knees while Daniel pressed a towel against his shoulder. The big man reached out a shaking hand. "Lucy—"

Raven placed her shaking fingers at Lucy's throat. "I feel a pulse. But barely."

Hondo cried out with grief. "Who did this?"

From a distance, a siren screamed toward them.

Raven met Daniel's gaze. "This is all my fault," she whispered. "If only I could remember and stop these people.

Blood soaked the second towel. Lucy was still. Too still.

"Don't give up," Raven begged. "Please don't. Hondo needs you."

Hondo sank to the floor, holding his sister's hand. "These animals don't deserve any mercy, Adams. You make sure my Lucy gets justice."

Daniel's face went hard. "I promise we'll get them, Hondo. I keep my promises, too. I'll find out who did this, and they'll pay. No matter what it takes."

Chapter Seven

The sun had fallen too far in the sky by the time the crime-scene team had come and gone. Daniel stuffed the last few personal items into his duffel while the doctor checked out Raven in the motel room next door. They'd be hard pressed to make it to the location he'd found when he had searched the satellite images of the area for a place to hole up.

The scent of blood permeated everywhere from the stain on the floor of room six where the paramedics had worked so hard to save Lucy. Her heart had stopped twice, and when they'd carried her out, her complexion was still gray.

Daniel had seen enough bullet injuries to know her chances weren't good. He didn't know whether Hondo would survive, either, but he knew if Lucy didn't make it, the man's life would be changed forever. Hondo had lived to protect his sister.

Nothing Daniel could say would ever change the reality that his choice to return to the motel may have cost two lives. Hondo had every right to hate him. If something like this were to happen to either one of his sisters, Daniel would lose it. He yanked the duffel bag's zipper closed, his frustration boiling deep inside.

The men who were after Raven didn't care who they hurt. Anyone who got between them and their objective was fair game. Daniel hadn't lied to Hondo. Their attackers deserved to die for what they'd done.

Sheriff Galloway stood in the doorway and scowled. "I don't like you taking off into parts unknown with no backup."

"Tough. We've got to disappear. Lucy's closer to dead than alive, and Hondo's not much better. You hired me for my expertise. Well, my gut says 'get the hell out of here.' I'm holing up in a place they can't find us. And if they do luck out, I'll defend Raven with whatever it takes." Daniel tucked the Glock in the back of his jeans. "I can't protect Raven here."

The only other way he could help her was to make use of his psychology degree and try the memory therapy. For that she needed quiet and safety. Daniel could use the open spaces to think. Yet they had to be close enough to Trouble, Texas, that they could return quickly, and since the town truly was hours from anywhere, that left one option.

"Which way are you heading?" Galloway asked, his voice low.

Daniel slung his duffel over his shoulder. "Sorry, Sheriff. The fewer who know the better."

Galloway slapped his Stetson against his leg. "How will I get in touch with you? What if I discover her identity?"

"Call Blake Redmond. I'll keep in touch with him," Daniel said. "That's the best I can do." He shoved his way past Galloway, scrutinized the surroundings, then tossed their meager belongings into the back of the truck beside the small satchel Noah had given him and the whip. His entire body on high alert, he searched once again. Though the clouds to the west had darkened the horizon, two hours of daylight were left. Daniel hoped it was enough.

The streets had been cordoned off due to the crime

scene. Galloway's young deputy stood watch. So far, so good.

Daniel returned to the neighboring room and stood in the doorway as the doctor finished his check on Raven.

"She okay?" he asked.

The gray-haired man scowled. "For someone who's been in a cave-in, an explosion and a drive-by, sure, she's great."

Daniel grimaced. "Now you know why we're leaving." He held out his hand to Raven. "You ready, darlin'?"

She rose. "How are Lucy and Hondo?" she asked.

"In surgery in El Paso," Sheriff Galloway said. "It's too soon to tell."

"Would you tell Hondo…" Raven gripped Daniel's hand like she clung to a lifeline. "Would you tell him I'm so very, very sorry? I wish…" Her voice trailed off. "I hope they'll be okay. I guess there's nothing else to say, is there?"

Daniel led her to the truck and helped her inside. Trouble looked at him expectantly. "Come on, boy. You get into the front seat for this ride. I think she needs you."

Trouble hopped onto the floorboard, and Raven scratched his ears.

Daniel shut the door on them and faced Galloway. "Thanks, Sheriff. I'll be in touch to resign when this is over."

Galloway ignored the comment. "Stay safe."

Daniel paused. "If you see Hondo, tell him we're both sorry. For everything. If he ever needs anything…I won't forget what happened today."

"I'll let him know when the time is right."

With one last stiff nod, Daniel slid into the driver's side and pulled out onto the highway. Raven sat quietly next to him, her hand buried in Trouble's fur as if the animal would keep her grounded. A mountain loomed in the distance to the west, the sun barely setting over its tall peaks.

"Where are we going?" Raven asked, her voice raw with emotion.

"There's a section of desert below Guadalupe Peak with several caves where we can find shelter and quiet," Daniel said. "I have a SAT phone. Noah and Elijah can get in touch if they discover something. If the CTC psychological program works, we can call them. But we'll be safe there."

He glanced in the rearview mirror and tugged hard at the vehicle, pulling off the road and behind a small bunch of juniper trees. With a quick move, he slid out his Glock and waited.

"What are you doing? Did you see someone?"

"No, but if we're being followed, this is the only way out of town. I'm taking no chances."

A few minutes passed. Not one car went by. Daniel glanced at his map and took off down a dirt road. The holes and rock roads jarred the truck. Daniel peered over the darkening landscape. He'd have to stop soon, but he wanted to put as much distance between them and Trouble, Texas, as possible.

"I don't think anyone *could* follow us, even if they wanted to," Raven said with a quick look behind them.

"That's the point." The final rays of dusk pierced the dust, exploding in color across a sea of rock and sand. No sign of civilization peeked up for miles in any direction.

"No distractions, that's certain," Daniel said, scanning her face with a concerned gaze. "Any dizziness left?" he asked.

She shook her head, and for the first time since he'd found her in that mine, he didn't see her wince. She pressed her fingers against the cut on her temple. "My head is still a little sore, but at least it doesn't feel like someone took a hammer to it anymore."

"Good." Daniel studied the dramatic rocks thrusting up from the earth. "The place we're heading will be quiet. It'll give you a chance to rest your mind."

"I may never be able to have peace again. Too much has happened," she said softly. "I don't know if I'll ever forget Lucy's look at me after she was shot. She hurt so bad," Raven said, her hand twisting the material of the latest pair of borrowed scrubs she wore.

"If I've learned anything over the past few months, it's that you can't forget. You can only try to live with what happened." He patted her hand. "You have the strength to do that, Raven. I know it."

Uncertainty clouded her expression—and something more.

"I can see a question in your eyes, Raven. What do you want to know?"

"Horrible things were done to you," she said softly. "I can't imagine. Do you think…do you think it'll ever be over for you?"

God, what a question. Unknowingly, the woman had flailed a layer of skin off his soul with her words. "I don't know."

Her gaze met his, and she nodded. "Thank you for being honest. It's one of the many reasons I trust you."

He cleared his throat. "Look, I'm not one to trust. I'm trained to deceive. In every assignment I dealt with men and women who had no consciences, who would lie, cheat or steal for money or power or a twisted view of the world." He stuffed his free hand in his pocket and toyed with the bullet casing.

"Then why do you keep doing your job? You sound like you hate it."

"Someone has to."

Her gaze narrowed with concern. "This CTC you keep mentioning—you work for them? How can they expect you—?"

"They want me to take a job. Right now I'm…" he paused "…on a leave of absence from my regular gig."

Her questions were getting too pointed. He shifted in his seat and checked the darkening sky. An outcropping of rock caught his attention, and he recognized the lay of the land. Maybe his luck was changing. "We're almost there." He pointed to a spot halfway up the side of a low mesa.

A flash of lightning pierced the blue-gray clouds, its jagged end snapping toward earth. A rumble of thunder followed the spark.

Large raindrops hit the windshield.

Trouble whined.

"Are we climbing up?" Raven asked.

"There's a four-wheel-drive path halfway up. We can't leave the truck down here. That last turn took us into a low-lying wash." The truck's headlights flashed against a rock face. "See the water-level mark. Flash floods can happen out here in no time."

"It's not raining that hard."

"Maybe not here but who knows up in those mountains. It doesn't happen often, but at this time of year, you can't be too careful."

By the time Daniel maneuvered the truck to higher ground and parked as close to the cave as he could get, the rain had started really coming down. "Who'd think we'd end up in a rainstorm in the deserts of West Texas? But it's too dark to change plans."

He slammed on his Stetson, ducked out of the truck, and then grabbed his equipment and the small bag of toys Noah had given him. His fingertips hesitated over the whip, but with a small curse, he grabbed it.

Noah knew him well. Daniel wouldn't let the duke win. A few hundred feet later, he stood in front of a shallow cave. At least he didn't have to search for occupants; he could see to the back. Thank God. No more dark, winding passages. He returned to Raven, opened the passenger door. Trouble jumped out of the truck and headed for shelter.

"Smart dog," Raven said.

"He's a survivor." Daniel led Raven to the cave. He unpacked a sleeping bag and the provisions Galloway had provided for them.

Within minutes they'd set up camp. A small hunting lantern illuminated the earthen room. Darkness had closed around them, but the night roared with thunder, and lightning streaked between the clouds and arced like daggers to the earth. Rain pummeled the dry ground, running in torrents off the side of the mesa into the wash.

"I wasn't expecting this," he said, raising his voice over the roar.

Raven huddled against the rock wall, hugged her arms to her body and shivered slightly. The temperature had cooled. Daniel pulled off his field jacket and wrapped it around her.

"Thank you." Raven smiled up at him in gratitude. His heart did a flip inside his chest. She knelt down and pulled out a protein bar. "Dinner?"

He snagged the food and sat just inside the cave's entrance, looking out at the rain. This position was safer—in so many ways. "We won't be leaving anytime soon," he said quietly. "With this much water, the ground would collapse from under us. Even the four-wheel drive will have trouble getting through these conditions."

"Which means no one can follow us," Raven said quietly. "We're safe."

He twisted to look at her vulnerable features. "Yes, you're safe." *Even from me.*

God, he hoped so.

Raven clasped the locket. "I wish I knew if the baby was."

What could he say? Daniel rubbed the nape of his neck to ease the tension. He focused on her face, doing his damnedest to ignore the three walls encroaching on him. The fresh air helped. At least his heart wasn't racing through his chest. Small rivulets of water dripped down his back, reminding him he wasn't being especially supportive. He was sitting half outside.

Raven sat alone at the back of the cave, looking small and desolate. He couldn't deny her need. Shoving aside his demons, he ducked inside, something he would never have done a few days ago. He settled next to her and wrapped his arms around her. "You're safe now," he repeated, pressing her trembling body close to his side. "Let's look at her photograph."

The flickering lantern bathed Raven's pale skin in light, illuminating her face. God, she truly was beautiful.

She released the locket's catch and opened the necklace. Noah had taken a few strands of the baby's hair and a copy of the photograph back to Carder for analysis, but he'd left some hair and the original snapshot.

Daniel had insisted. Raven needed the connection those few strands gave her. He knew that. When everything was taken away, somehow you had to find one concrete belief to hold on to. Raven's belief was that the child in the locket was her baby.

Raven's brow furrowed in concentration, and her fingertips touched the edge of the image. "Look at those innocent eyes. They give me hope," Raven said softly, glancing up at him. "Hope. It's strange, but the word makes my heart warm. Maybe I haven't truly lost it."

Her lashes fluttered closed. She leaned against him, and he focused on the feel of her body pressing close. The walls had stopped closing him in, and a small fire of optimism kindled inside. Maybe he was healing a bit.

Raven stirred. "Something tells me I wanted her very badly," she said. "Like I waited a long time for her."

She blinked, swaying back and forth, a small hum escaping from her lips that was barely audible over the storm outside. He leaned his head closer to her lips. A lullaby, perhaps?

"Ashes, ashes," she sang. "We all fall down." Her body stilled. "I don't know how I know, but I hate that song. It gives me chills." Her shoulders sagged, and she opened her eyes. "For a moment something was there. Something bad. Then it vanished."

"Every day the flashes become more frequent," he said, pulling her even closer.

"I miss her so much. How can I when I don't even remember her? I'm so scared I won't remember in time," she said, frustration mounting. "I feel like I'm failing her."

He turned Raven into his arms. "You are not a failure." He cupped her cheek, unable to look away from her. "You are courageous and brave and caring." His voice turned hoarse at the words. "In fact, you amaze me."

Her pupils dilated, turning her cinnamon-colored eyes dark with awareness. His body tensed. Everything inside of him wanted to lean into her, to touch her, to hold her, not in comfort but in something much more dangerous.

"This probably isn't a good idea," he muttered, even as his body strained against his jeans. He couldn't resist. He leaned into her.

His thumb rubbed against her full lower lip. Her mouth parted. Raven raised her hand to his scarred cheek. "You're a good man, Daniel Adams, but I don't need you to protect me. Not from this."

Her tongue teased the pad of his thumb. His body tightened against his zipper, and he swallowed.

"Kiss me," she whispered.

He couldn't stop himself even if he'd wanted to. He lowered his mouth to hers, gingerly, gently, softly, though every part of him screamed to yank her close. He teased her lips with his mouth, dancing over them until they parted under his caress.

A groan rumbled in his throat. He brought her closer to him. Her breasts crushed against his chest, and his hands explored her back, up to her head, pressing her closer. She let out a small whimper and put a hand to her bandaged forehead.

He released her immediately. "I hurt you," he said. "I should have known." He slid away.

"My scalp's just a little tender," she said, her breathing coming fast. She leaned forward. "Don't stop."

Daniel took a shuddering breath. His hand reached behind him and encountered the whip he'd tossed into the cave. He sighed as the passion left him, and reality returned. "It's not a good idea. Whatever is happening between us, it's not real, Raven. It's just the crazy circumstances."

Her eyes cleared. "I may not know my name, Daniel, but I know what's real." She gestured between them. "This is real. You may not like it, but it's definitely real."

He shoved his hand through his hair. "Look, I can't hide that I want you, or that I crave a lot more than a kiss from you. We both know it would be easy to just let go, to escape for a while, but..." Daniel clutched the whip and held it before him. “Even if you remembered everything, I have baggage I won’t saddle you with.”

She stared at the coiled leather in his hand. “What’s that for?” she whispered, a trace of fear in her voice.

“Therapy,” Daniel said, curling his hand around the handle. “It’s the whip my captor, the Duke of Sarbonne, used in Bellevaux. Noah gave it to me before he left. As a present.”

“That seems cruel. Why would he do that to you?”

“Because I dream about that whip,” Daniel bit out, his voice hard. “Every night. You need your memories back, Raven. I’d give anything for my memories of that time to be erased forever.”

Lightning cracked outside, and Daniel winced. “Because sounds like that can send me back to that dungeon in seconds. My PTSD makes my back burn as if the bastard were whipping me right now.” He shifted his shoulder and then rose until his head nearly hit the roof of the cave. “Get some rest, Raven. I’ll be outside.” He paused. “Maybe Noah is right. It’s time to exorcise some demons.”

“Let me help you. Let me comfort you like you’ve comforted me. I’m a good listener.” She held out her hand to him. “Stay with me.”

He frowned at her, then looked back at the rain pouring down. At least the thunder and lightning were moving on. “I can’t stay. Not until I’m certain I’m not a demon myself.”

CHRISTOPHER LEANED BACK in the driver’s side of the SUV and stared at the ramshackle house on the darkened street just on the edge of the war zone in El Paso.

“You sure this is her house?” he asked Tad. “It’s a dump.”

His friend popped a wad of chewing tobacco into his cheek. “No mistake. I got a good friend at the phone company. She looked her up for me." Tad gripped his crotch. "She got a little extra for her effort. Good thing she likes it rough."

Christopher shook his head. "You really are a depraved SOB. Did you get rid of the body?"

"Nah. I didn't kill her. Thought about it, but women who like it my way are hard to find."

Christopher opened the SUV door. "Well, now that the bitch who tried to steal my baby sister is finally dead, I can start my life over. Wait here."

"Yeah, yeah. Hurry up. It's hot as hell still, even if it is night," Tad muttered, tugging his phone from his pocket. "I'll check some porn sites while you're gone." He smirked and kicked up a heel on the dashboard.

Christopher shook his head. Sometimes he didn't know about Tad's taste in women. None of his friend's relationships were like what he had with Chelsea. She'd saved his sanity. Christopher had hated growing up in the middle of nowhere—except for the hunting—until he'd found Chelsea. Back then she'd lived in Van Horn, only an hour away. He'd loved her the moment he saw her at a high school football game, dark hair blowing in the wind, green eyes sparkling. He should have written more, but she'd still be glad to see him.

His heart thudded against his chest, eagerness adding a spring to his step. He walked up the sidewalk, scanning right, then left. Habit from his military training. An old woman peered through her front window, then quickly closed the curtains. People knew better than to get involved in this neighborhood.

The first thing he'd do is get Chelsea out of here. They'd move into the big house with his mom and sister. Chelsea deserved a nice house. She could help take care of the baby in preparation for their own family.

He smiled at the image, placed his hand on the doorknob and tested it. The lock jiggled. Dangerous for this area.

Christopher knocked softly. Padded footsteps creaked across the floor. A curtain loosely fluttered.

He banged again.

"Chelsea, honey, it's me. Christopher. I'm home."

She didn't open the door.

His body tensed; his jaw tightened. "Chelsea. It's me. Open up," he said, his voice low and urgent.

The floor creaked near the door. What the hell was she doing? He'd imagined this day from the moment he'd been forced to redeploy. They'd cancelled his leave twice for disciplinary actions. It had been too long, and this wasn't the way homecoming worked.

He pounded on the wooden door over and over and over again. "I'm back. Just like I promised. Damn it, let me in, Chelsea." His temper erupted, and he let his fist fly. The wood cracked beneath the force.

He stood back, ready to kick it in, when the door creaked open, and Chelsea's terrified face peeked out.

"Chris…Christopher. I…I thought you were still overseas."

"Yeah, well, things changed." In one move he shoved into the house. "Why didn't you open the door for me?" He grabbed her by the hair and tilted her head back. "Is someone here? Is that why you wouldn't answer?"

"No, of course not. I…just…" she licked her lips, and her gaze darted left "…couldn't believe it was you. There's no one here, Christopher. I promise."

Eyes darting left was a sure sign of a lie. Christopher shoved her away then slammed through the small house, checking every room.

Empty.

His heart thudded with fury that had no way to expend itself. Why did she always do this? Get him worked up when she didn't have to. He sucked in several deep breaths and walked into the living room. She cowered in the corner.

Immediately remorse washed over him. "I'm sorry, baby. The war got to me. It was ugly, and I've just missed you so much."

He grabbed her arms and pulled her close, tucking her against his chest. He needed sex, and he needed it now. Nothing else would take the edge off.

She shivered against him, and a small sob escaped.

He caressed her hair. "It's okay, honey. Everything's all right. I'm back. I'm here now. Things will be like they were before. Just you and me."

He picked her up and carried her into the bedroom. "How about a welcome home?"

Her eyes went wide. "But…but…"

He frowned. "Don't you want me?"

"I…uh…I don't have protection."

"You don't have to worry about that, sweetie. We don't need it. I want to have babies with you. I always have."

Ten minutes later he sat up, sated but irritated.

"What's wrong?" he demanded. "Why were you crying?"

"N…nothing's wrong. Just…I'm…happy you're back." She stared at the wall, at a painting of a woman alone on the beach, but tears wet her cheeks.

"You women are nuts. Tad's waiting for me, but I'll be back." He touched her face. "You'll never be alone again. We'll be together forever, Chelsea. We'll be so happy together."

He kissed her, and left her soft and warm in bed, making sure to lock the front door behind him.

He couldn't stop smiling and slid into the SUV.

"You look satisfied." Tad frowned. "Didn't take long."

"Been a while." Christopher grinned. He leaned back in his seat with a sigh. "It's been a good day. I got my girl back. I'm home and have Dad's money waiting for me. My baby sister is safe." He flipped on the radio. "Our little shootout should have made the news by now."

The newscaster's voice droned through the radio. "And big city problems have made their way into the tiny West Texas town of Trouble. A drive-by shooting left one woman clinging to life, and her brother seriously injured. More updates as information is made available, but sources close to the investigation have identified the victims as William 'Hondo' Rappaport and his sister, Lucy Rappaport Hardiman."

Christopher jerked and slammed his hand on the dash. "Damn you, Tad. You took out the wrong targets. That woman is still alive!"

WATER SOAKED DANIEL'S jeans and T-shirt, but he didn't care. He couldn't feel the rain. He stared out at the thunderstorm, waiting for another snap of lightning. It was far enough away that he might not get struck by it. If it weren't for Raven, he wasn't sure he'd care.

With the whip in his hand, every crack triggered the memories. His mind whirled between the past and the present, but he pushed the dungeon away until he knew he stood at the edge of the wash. In Texas.

Daniel tightened his grip, the seal digging into his palm. He wouldn't let the bastard win.

A flash of lightning.

The clap of thunder.

Daniel lifted his arm. He cracked the whip over the edge. The leather snapped in the air.

The roar of thunder rolled through the night. He stared into the eerie flickering of the sky. One glance over his shoulder, and the dim light from the cave glowed like a beacon. Raven was in there. Afraid, vulnerable, huddled with Trouble, and here he was, playing with a whip.

"You won't beat me, Sarbonne!" he yelled into the night. Thunder crashed, and Daniel flicked the whip. Again and again and again. "You won't control me. I won't let you."

Rain ran down his face. His eyes burned. He might have cried. He couldn't tell. He lifted his arm again, and again, and again. Each crack drove a hole into the memories choking him. He lost himself in the desperation to annihilate his past.

"You don't control me anymore, you bastard."

Hour after hour passed until Daniel could barely lift his arm, when finally, finally, he didn't wince, his back didn't burn.

He glared into the retreating storm. Rain still pelted his face, stinging his cheeks, but the worst was over. He stared at the whip in his hand. The whip was just a whip.

Thank you, Noah.

For a moment, he considered tossing the monstrosity into the wash. He turned it over and over in his hand.

Another slash of lightning lit the sky, reflected off the Sarbonne crest. Daniel tensed, but got his emotions under control.

One demon down. Daniel yelled into the night, "You won't win. I won't let you."

His body sagged. He bent over, hands on his knees, and sucked in several deep breaths, then slowly repeated, "I won't let you."

RAVEN HUDDLED IN the mouth of the small cave and stared at Daniel through the darkness. A distant flash of lightning illuminated his features. Now exhaustion replaced the stark pain carved on his face.

He stood and looked up into the sky, his shoulders shaking with a depth of release she could barely comprehend. Tears flowed undaunted down her cheeks. She couldn't get the haunted expression he'd worn out of her mind.

He stood frozen in the rain, the water sluicing over him. Every instinct urged her to go to him, to comfort him, to wrap her arms around him and give him strength.

He was so alone. So horribly, painfully alone, but she didn't move. Daniel had pushed her away once.

Did that make her a coward?

Trouble stood just inside the cave, whining forlornly. He looked ready to leap at Daniel, but even he hesitated.

"He saved us, Trouble. What do we do?" The mutt looked up at her with a sad expression. She stood.

She took off Daniel's jacket.

Her heart aching, she stepped into the storm. Within seconds her clothes were drenched and clung to her skin. Her feet slipped on the mud, and she flailed awkwardly but didn't fall. Her entire focus remained on the man standing at the edge of an abyss she couldn't fathom.

He was alone.

He wouldn't be for long.

She took a shuddering breath and stepped closer. Daniel didn't turn around. He might not even know she'd left the cave. She hesitated.

The roar of the storm circled around them, but somehow he sensed her presence.

"You shouldn't have come in the rain, Raven," he said, his voice hoarse. "Go back inside."

"No." She slipped her arms around his waist and leaned her cheek against his broad shoulders. She hugged him tight, needing him to know she was there. "I won't leave you."

At her words, a shiver ran through his body. He placed his hands on hers. At first she thought he might pry her away, but then he let out a low groan and gripped her tight.

"I don't have the will to fight you," he said, his voice harsh with grief. He turned to her. "If you don't want me to make love to you, walk away. I won't follow."

She slid her hands lower, past his belt to the proof of his desire.

"So be it." Daniel scooped her up and cradled her against his chest. "There's no turning back now."

Chapter Eight

Raven ignored the rain. She simply wrapped her hands around Daniel's neck and clung to him. His strong arms nestled her closer. She tucked her head against his chest, his steady heart thudding in time with his quick steps. Within seconds he stepped beneath the rock outcropping into a haven from the storm. Her vision blurred, she barely noticed Trouble slinking into the corner of the cave and curling up.

Slowly Daniel set her to her feet. His hands were wet but warm on her face. His gaze hypnotized her, his eyes blazing with heat and passion and something untamed and wild.

Her breath caught in her throat, and she couldn't look away. She couldn't move; she could only stare, held fast by the intensity of him. Her lips went dry, and she moistened them with her tongue.

"Last chance," he whispered, his voice deep and husky, almost a growl.

Something about the storm outside and the tempest swirling deep inside her froze her in his arms. She wanted to be with him. She wanted to feel his strength. Everywhere. Holding her, touching her, claiming her.

She said nothing, but met his gaze, unwavering in her

certainty. She closed her eyes and leaned into him, lifting her lips to his. "I want you."

Daniel growled deep in his chest, but he didn't kiss her, just encircled her with his strong arms, holding her tenderly, close, as if she were the most precious thing in the world.

"You're vulnerable," he said.

Raven leaned slightly, grabbed at his belt and anchored him close. "Daniel Adams, you are not backing out now." She wrapped her arms around his waist and stood on tiptoes to whisper in his ear. "I may not remember everything," she said softly, "but I do know I want this."

No demands. No looking for commitments later. Just you and me finding solace in the storm.

She kissed the line of his jaw, relishing the feel of its whisker-rough edge. "I want you."

Lightning split the sky. Thunder roared. "I can't resist you," he said finally.

His hands cupped her backside. Daniel lifted her off her feet, and she wrapped her legs around his hips and her arms around his neck, holding tight. He nipped her throat, and Raven tilted her head back, giving him access to the hypersensitive skin.

In two steps Daniel pressed her against the wall of the cave. She could feel the rocks through her shirt, but she didn't care. She clutched at his hair and let out a soft gasp. He took his time, wooing her skin with kisses, exploring the pulse point at her neck, then moving lower. He nibbled at the top of her breasts and shoved aside her shirt, hitching her higher, and feasted on her curves, his mouth working magic wherever he explored.

Her head dropped back against the cave wall, and she audibly sighed. "Please," she panted. "Don't make me wait."

She could barely catch her breath. She clutched his head between her hands and bent down. Finally, her lips met his.

There was nothing tentative or new in their kiss. His mouth crushed hers, invading her very being, and she welcomed him. Uncertainty had claimed everything in her life. Except for her need for the man in her arms.

She tightened her legs around him. He took her lips again, telling her without words how much he wanted her.

The world fell away as his mouth and hands seduced her body and soul. She couldn't hear or smell or feel anything. Except Daniel.

He lifted his lips from hers, then stared into her eyes. She clutched his arms, shaking with want, needing him to douse the fire burning her skin. "Please," she whispered, trembling in his arms.

His gaze unwavering, he gently lowered them both to the sleeping bag. His eyes flickered in the light of the lantern. He trailed his finger down her jaw. "You're beautiful."

"So are you." She let her touch flutter against the scar on his cheek. He flinched, but her hand remained steady. "I love your strength and courage."

He went to speak, but she stopped him with a finger to his lips. "Shh." She pushed him, and he let her roll him to his back, then she straddled him. Her wet hair framed her face, and her hips shifted on top of his.

His eyes darkened. She lifted the scrub shirt over her head and unhooked her bra. She felt brazen but powerful. He couldn't take his eyes away from her. He cupped her breasts in his hands.

Raven leaned down and let her breasts press against his chest. "Take me now." She pressed her lips against his and then explored his mouth. "Now. That's an order."

Suddenly he laughed. "I don't always follow orders well," Daniel said, flipping her onto her back. "But this time..." His teeth teased her nipple until she arched against him. "This time, nothing will stop me."

He pressed a denim-clad leg between hers and explored her naked torso with his hands and mouth. She didn't know how he removed the remainder of their clothes so quickly, but suddenly he settled on top of her, and he was touching her everywhere. With devastating thoroughness, he worked his way down one leg, then up the other until he found the center of her. She cried out as he caressed her, and her body exploded in an eruption of need. She could feel his throbbing heat, strong and hard and wanting. "Daniel," she panted. "I want you inside me."

In response, he grabbed the bag Noah had provided and dug into the side pocket. She whimpered in protest until he pulled out a foil packet.

He slipped on the condom and held himself above her. Her heart raced until she thought it might leap from her chest, then he shifted, joining them as one. She cried out in joyous relief.

His eyelids fluttered closed. For a few moments he remained unmoving, sucking in one breath, then another.

She wrapped herself around him, tilting her hips, cradling him, surrounding him. They belonged together. She wanted to whisper the words, but she didn't dare.

As if he had heard her, Daniel let out a low moan. "God, it's like coming home."

A wall seemed to crumble between them. He lowered his mouth to hers and moved against her, driving her higher and higher until she called out into the night, her mind and heart flying free for the first time since he'd found her.

CHRISTOPHER HAD WANTED to push his vehicle to the limits to return to Trouble, but he couldn't risk anyone stopping him, so he'd gone the speed limit. He and Tad set up on the outskirts of town. Now Christopher paced back and forth beside the SUV. The grumble of thunder sounded in the distance, over the mountain, making the hair on the back of his neck stand at attention.

Static crackled from the listening device he'd placed at the sheriff's office. He shoved his boot heel into the ground and let out a string of curses; then he whirled and slammed his fist into the vehicle's side. "Damn it. What's taking so long? I was sure Galloway would know, or at least get in touch with that woman. Where the hell is she?"

Tad shoved his hand through his hair. "You never did have any patience for surveillance. It's just another part of the hunt. She'll turn up sooner or later."

Christopher rounded on his friend and grabbed him by the neck. "Listen to me. I'm protecting my family, and if I have to kill someone to do it, I will. Even you. So shut up and let me think."

A sharp ring sounded through the speaker. Chris shoved Tad away and turned up the volume.

"Sheriff. This is Noah Bradford. I'm trying to reach Daniel. I have news, and I need to talk to him. I can't get through to his SAT phone."

"Sorry, Bradford, but Adams left without telling me where they were going. Didn't trust that we could protect Raven. Not that I blame him," Galloway complained. "Lucy's still touch-and-go. Hondo's in a bad way. I'd get the hell out, too."

Noah swore succinctly. "I'm sorry about your friends, but I've got to talk to him. There's a tracer in his laptop so I have his coordinates. If I give them to you, can you get to him immediately?"

"Yeah, won't be a problem."

The man named Noah read off the digits.

"Jackpot." Christopher grabbed a pen from Tad and wrote the information on his arm.

Galloway whistled. "I just checked the map. Not good. They're by the washes that lead away from the peak. There's a flash flood warning for that area. The place is unstable at the best of times, but with the unexpected rain in the mountains, the ground there won't soak up anything. There will be flash floods and mudslides all over that land. Even if I wanted to get to him, he has the four-wheel drive. I can't risk it with the vehicles I have. Maybe dirt bikes could get in."

"Forget it." Noah let out another curse. "I'm taking a chopper to get them out."

"What's going on, Bradford?" Sheriff Galloway asked, his voice suspicious.

"That's the problem, Sheriff. We have no idea, but I've got a really bad feeling this is where the whole case is about to change."

The call ended.

Christopher grinned. "Damn straight." He and Tad jumped in the SUV. "It took a few hours, but it paid off, Tad. We know where they are now, and I got an easy way to make that woman's death look like an accident."

"Now let's go steal some dirt bikes."

DANIEL'S HEART RACED like he'd just run for his life, but he felt like he'd grabbed a small piece of heaven. He didn't want to leave the warmth of Raven's body. She lay curled against him with her eyes closed, but she wasn't asleep. Her grip on him was too strong, as if she didn't want to let him go.

An unfamiliar warmth seeped through his chest, surrounding his heart. He kissed the top of her hair and stared out into the night. It felt so right to have Raven in his arms.

He tucked her head under his chin, being careful not to bump her wound.

She sighed and wriggled closer. “Thank you,” she whispered, her voice low.

He smiled and tightened his hold. “That should be my line.”

She laughed. “In that case, you’re welcome.”

She shifted in his arms and looked up at him, the flickering of the lantern illuminating her dark hair, creating a halo around her head.

He pushed back the silky locks. How he wished he could have been there to protect her from the beginning. She should never have been so vulnerable. Her bruises hadn’t faded much, and she couldn’t hide the circles of fatigue under her eyes, but she was the most beautiful woman he’d ever known, because her beauty came from deep inside.

“I haven’t felt like a normal woman since I woke up,” she whispered. “Not until now.”

“Normal is overrated,” Daniel teased, even as his body hardened against hers. “Your uniqueness is way better than that. I like the sounds you make when I’m inside you.”

A soft blush reddened her cheeks, and he smiled, feeling halfway human for the first time since Bellevaux. A flashing image of the black bag being pulled over his head and him being dragged into that prison cell seared his mind. He didn’t want to think about his past.

No.

He hated the memories. He wouldn’t let them taint this moment.

Daniel let his fingertips linger against the bruise on her temple. “Head still okay?”

“Fine,” she said with a small yawn.

He kissed her temple. “Try to get some sleep. I won’t

leave you," he said, settling her against him. "I'll keep you safe."

Her eyelids fluttered close. "Safe," she said. "I like feeling safe."

After several minutes, her breathing grew regular.

Daniel didn't want to move. He wanted to just disappear in this cave forever with Raven, but she shifted onto her side, and the lantern's light reflected off the locket around her neck, reminding him that disappearing wasn't an option.

In fact, ignoring the past wasn't an option.

For either of them.

PAMELA STARED AT the baby in the crib, her cheeks rosy and healthy. The other baby. If Chelsea had given her this one, everything would have been fine.

Now Pamela loved Christina with an obsession that scared even her.

The little girl whimpered and let out a sneeze.

No. This baby couldn't get sick. They'd call off the procedure. That wouldn't work.

Christina was failing faster.

Pamela raced down the hall and grabbed a vaporizer. Within twenty minutes the room was bathed in healing steam. She paced back and forth, every few seconds staring down at the child.

Christopher hadn't come home, thank God. She'd seen the wild look in his eyes and recognized he hadn't changed. Somehow she had to figure out a way to get away from him without him learning the truth about the babies.

A ringing phone pierced the night. Pamela ran into the hallway and picked up the receiver. "Hello?"

Small sobs sounded through the line. "Mrs. W...Winter?"

A chill skittered down Pamela's back. "Chelsea? You

promised never to call. You promised to disappear. We had a deal."

"And you promised me Christopher would never find me after I moved this time. That the baby would be safe. I never should have let you take her. I should have given them both to…" Her voice trailed off. "He'll find out, and he'll kill me."

Pamela gritted her teeth. Quietly she shut the door to the nursery and walked into her bedroom. She stared at the photograph of her husband, a picture to remind her of one truth. A truth it had taken her thirty years to understand. Mercy didn't win. Only power won—and witnesses weren't to be left behind.

"You have to do something." Chelsea sobbed. "He came here tonight. He…he wants me back. He wants babies with me. I can't let that happen."

"Did you upset him?" Pamela asked, shifting her feet back and forth, her gaze snapping to the photo of her husband once again. "Why did you even let him in your house?"

"I didn't know he was back. I looked through the window, and he saw me. You could have warned me. You know how he can get. I had to… I let him…" Chelsea choked back another sob. "I didn't dare risk him flying into one of his rages."

Pamela tapped her chin. She probably should have warned Christopher's old girlfriend, but the woman had betrayed her, too. A sudden thought occurred to Pamela. She rose and peeked into the nursery. What if she told Christopher about the babies using Chelsea as a scapegoat? Yes. The plan might just work. If she played it smart, she could solve two problems with one small revelation. Chelsea's call may have been the answer to her prayers.

"Help me?" Chelsea said.

Pamela drummed her fingers on the phone. She couldn't reveal her intentions. She had to string Chelsea along. "What can I do? He doesn't listen to me, either." She let her voice shake, made herself sound vulnerable. She'd certainly borne the brunt of her husband's and then Christopher's anger. She had no intention of going through that again.

"You know enough to put him behind bars. The cops will believe his mother. You can tell everyone about what he's done. About his *hunting* trips. About the kid who went missing in the wash ten years ago. I want Christopher put away. I want the baby safe. I want to be free."

"You're right." Pamela took one last look at the sleeping child in the bed. "I know exactly what to do, Chelsea. You won't have to worry anymore. I'll take care of everything."

RAVEN FLOATED ABOVE the vision: a long flowing white dress. A church. A handsome man at her side—but not Daniel. Oh, God, a man she didn't know. A man with blond hair, too handsome to be real. She had to be dreaming. Rings were exchanged, then kisses.

No. This was wrong. It couldn't be a wedding. She shook her head, wanting the images to vanish. She wanted to stay warm and loved in Daniel's arms, but those strange impressions felt real. Felt true.

She cried out, devastated, even in sleep.

"Raven, wake up. You're having a nightmare. You're okay, darlin'." Daniel held her wrists, one leg thrown across her waist. "You're with me."

Daniel's calm voice shattered the images in thousands of pieces, but her heart wouldn't stop pounding.

Blinking against the glare of the morning light, Raven looked down at her nude body and then stared at her left hand. No ring. No tan lines revealing she'd even worn one. Yet she couldn't shake the certainty in her soul that the dream was real.

"I think I'm married," she whispered.

Daniel released her wrists, rolled off her and sat up. Tension emanated from his body. He tugged on his jeans and handed her a clean set of scrubs. "You're basing this on your dream?"

"It didn't feel like a dream, more like a memory." She quickly slipped into the clothes, hating that she couldn't have stayed naked in his arms, with nothing between them. She'd felt so close to him, and now a chasm wider than the wash separated them.

"We both knew this was a possibility," Daniel said. "I never should have touched you last night. God, I knew better. I'm sorry."

The words hurt, even though she expected them. "How can I feel what I do for you if I'm...?"

Her voice trailed off. She couldn't meet his gaze. "God, this is all so crazy." She rubbed her eyes with shaking hands. "I have to remember. I can't go on like this."

"You may not like what we discover," Daniel said. He raised his hand to her cheek, then dropped it before he touched her skin. "We should work on expanding some of your memories today."

"I know." She bit her lip, longing for a connection with Daniel, even though she shouldn't. "I watched you fight to control your memories. I have to fight to retrieve mine. For my baby. And for...myself."

"Okay, then." Daniel gave her a tight smile.

He opened Noah's satchel and pulled out a laptop and a smaller bag. He set the items between them.

"What's all this?"

"The CTC program I mentioned. I think it's worth a try, but I have to warn you, it may not be easy."

Daniel reached into the bag. "Sit back against the cave wall and relax. I have a number of items. Hold them, smell them, use your five senses to see if they trigger any images, any impressions." One by one he pulled out a baby's rattle, a pink blanket, baby shampoo and several toys.

She drew in a sharp breath. "My head is pounding already. Just looking at these toys makes my heart ache."

"Take it slow. You're safe here. Close your eyes. Let your mind wander."

He handed her the rattle, and she clutched it tight.

"Nothing."

"Try the shampoo. You had a reaction to the scent before," he said.

She did and her stomach heaved, her heart tripping in panic, but no new images appeared in her mind.

For over an hour, Daniel took her through the CTC program. Finally, when an image flashed on the screen for the third time with nothing to show for it but a headache, Raven jumped to her feet. "This is ridiculous. Nothing's coming back to me. I'm pushing and pushing, and my head is going to explode."

Her eyes burned with unshed tears.

She whirled around and stared at the gray sky outside. "We're wasting our time here. I'd rather sit in that clinic as bait, waiting until that maniac comes after me. *He* knows who I am. If we trap him, I have a chance of finding out, too."

She stalked out of the cave and walked to the edge of the wash. The suffocating loneliness of the desert settled over her. She wrapped her arms around her body, shaking. What if she never remembered? What if she never knew who she was or what happened to her baby? Could she live with that?

No, it would kill her.

She stared down into the wash, and a wave of despair, deep and dark, slammed against her.

Storm clouds gathered over the western mountains. Thunder sounded and lightning flashed some distance away, but the ground began to rumble, a roar coming ever closer. She peered over the wash just as a huge wall of water raced down the rock ravine.

Daniel ran out of the cave, the whip in his hand. "It's a flash flood. Get back."

She whirled around, but water splashed over the rocks and debris, slamming into the earthen ledge where she stood. The ground behind her gave way. She dove toward a mesquite tree growing out of rock and grabbed hold of one of its branches. The bark cut into her hands but she held tight, panting.

Frantic, she looked down at the swirling water. If she fell, she wouldn't survive. "Daniel!"

"Just hang on."

Without hesitation, Daniel tied one end of the long whip around the mesquite trunk and secured the other end to his belt to anchor himself. She was so close. If he could only reach her. He leaned toward her and grabbed one hand, but her wet fingers slipped from his grip.

The bark peeled off under her other hand and she closed her eyes, certain she would be swept away when Daniel managed to snag her wrist. His face strained, he began to pull her up, but to her horror, the earth beneath his feet started to crumble. He moved back and dug his heels into the dirt, but his body tilted off balance, leaning at an angle over the flood.

The churning torrent sped just below her feet now, but that could change at any second. A barbed wire fence careened through the water, its wooden stakes and wire a deadly weapon. The debris slammed against the earth. If they fell in, they were dead.

Trouble barked furiously, but the dog could do nothing.

"What are we going to do?" she shouted. Daniel tightened his hold on her wrist.

"I'm going to swing you toward the thicker branches over there. When you land, crawl up the trunk then get as far away from the edge as you can!" Daniel yelled.

She nodded.

"Okay, let go," he ordered.

With a prayer, she did, putting her life in Daniel's hand. He groaned and twisted his torso. She swung once, twice. "Now!" he shouted. He let go, and she landed on some thick branches and climbed toward the edge.

Suddenly the dirt shifted beneath Daniel's feet, and he dropped. He grabbed the whip and started hauling himself up.

Raven had crawled toward the cave but turned back. Trouble grabbed her shirt and pulled, dragging her to safety. She struggled against the dog's hold. "Daniel!"

"Stay back." Hand over hand, muscles straining, he clawed his way to the top. More ground gave way. He slid back until he was waist deep in the water. Another tree churned in the flood, heading straight for him.

"Look out!" she yelled.

He twisted just in time for a large branch to slam into his belly. His hands gripped the leather tighter, but the current pummeled him against the dirt and rock. Only the whip kept him from being swept away.

She had to do *something.*

Raven ran to the cave and dumped out Daniel's duffel. She found a climbing rope and ran outside, frantically searching for something to tie the cord on to that wasn't about to be swept away.

Suddenly the *whoop-whoop-whoop* of rotor blades sounded from above. A wave of air knocked her backwards, and she dropped the rope. A military-style helicopter swooped down toward Daniel.

A man wearing a dark cap and sunglasses leaned out with a weapon and shouted something, then raised his rifle.

"No!" Raven screamed.

Chapter Nine

The helicopter's blades forced a downdraft that threw Daniel off balance and buffeted him toward the water. Desperate, he grabbed a tree branch, using it and the whip to climb back up. The rotor blast stung his eyes. He tightened his grip, and the leather from the whip cut into his hands, the sting sharp as it bit into his palm. If he let go, he was dead.

What the hell was Noah doing here in the CTC chopper? Elijah fired a few rounds from the semiautomatic out the side door. As the helicopter turned, angling to hover near, Daniel braced himself for another gust then fought against the rush of man-made wind.

Damn idiots were going to drown him.

He couldn't let go of the whip. He'd fall. No one could survive the swirling water below. He'd be slammed against the rocks at high speed. If the blows didn't kill him, drowning would.

The helo dove again, really low, almost as if trying to skirt the water. Daniel whipped around to see what they were doing, but Elijah's attention was far from Daniel.

Elijah's line of sight led straight to the flat mesa about fifteen feet above the outcropping.

Two figures held automatic weapons pointed directly at Raven.

Daniel crawled higher, and the tree limb bent precariously lower. He had no time left. With a curse he rammed his boot into the broken branches then, hands bleeding, he pulled himself onto solid ground with the whip. His leg throbbed—hell, his whole body did—but he scrambled to Raven. He shielded her, then shoved her into the protection of the cave.

Gunfire peppered the exact spot where she'd been.

He felt Raven's heart pounding, but no faster than his own. "Stay here." He grabbed his weapon and bolted to the cave entrance.

Elijah sent off another round of gunfire toward the mesa. Two heads ducked down.

Daniel scanned the terrain for a way to get to the bastards. A small path caught his attention. It might take some climbing. He grasped a handhold, but the sandstone crumbled. With all the rain, he couldn't count on a good hold. Suddenly the chopper flew up several feet, and Elijah raised his weapon, but before he could fire, a spray of bullets pelted the helicopter. The chopper reeled away, but an arc of fluid spewed from near the tail.

Daniel's heart stopped as the chopper swiveled out of control and pitched toward the outcropping. They were going down.

Elijah hung on to a safety strap, then with fury in his eyes, sent one last burst of gunfire. A man fell from the mesa to the ground.

Trouble bolted across the terrain at the bleeding man, who crawled toward his weapon.

The man lunged for his gun, but Trouble leaped on him, growling. The dog grabbed hold of the guy's arm, clamping down. He cursed, twisting against the animal, rolling toward the edge, but Trouble wouldn't let go.

"Stop," Daniel called out. "You're going to fall." He

snagged the dropped rope from the ground at his feet and tossed it at the second gunman.

The guy ignored him, trying to break the dog's tight grip.

The man struggled to stand, but the ground gave way. He and Trouble tumbled into the rage of water.

"Trouble!" Raven ran toward the cave opening. A loud explosion rent the air, and a blast of heat seared the cave.

Oh, God, had Noah and Elijah made it out?

"Stay put. I have to check the helicopter!" Daniel shouted, waving Raven back. "There's a second gunman."

Raven's frantic gaze whipped around, taking in the horrific fireball. In the distance, a motorcycle engine revved, then faded away.

Daniel raced to the wash's edge, searching for Noah and Elijah. The only way they would have survived was if they had jumped into the floodwaters. Some choice. Burn or drown.

He caught sight of Noah's dark head bobbing, then Elijah's blond one. They fought to reach a long flat rock perched a third of the way into the wash. There was a small plateau nearby, just above water level. If Noah and Elijah could get to it, they might have a chance.

Daniel whirled around. "We need another rope..."

Raven was already digging into his duffel. She pulled out the second climbing rope.

"Hurry," he said. "They don't have much time."

Daniel and Raven raced along the crumbling edge of the wash, and he searched the chaotic maelstrom.

Trouble's body was wedged against a thick log, and he struggled to stay afloat.

"Trouble!" Raven screamed.

"I see him. He's heading for the rock."

"We have to help him," she said, then her face paled,

and her hand clamped to her mouth. "Is that Noah?" Raven asked, pointing.

Daniel followed her gaze. A dark-headed man's body bobbed facedown in the water. Noah? It couldn't be. Not after surviving four tours and countless missions.

The man's body smashed off a rock and flipped onto his back. Daniel let out a relieved sigh. "It's not him. It's the shooter who fell from the edge."

Even at thirty feet, Daniel could tell the gunman was dead. He couldn't see his eyes, but the guy had barbed wire wrapped around him and a steel rod impaling him through his chest.

"Stand on that rock. You'll have a good view. Keep Noah and Elijah in your sights and point them out," Daniel said. "I'm going to help them."

She gripped his hand. "Be careful. Please."

"Always, darlin'." He looped the rope over his shoulder. The water moved fast. If it rose much higher the cave would be flooded, as well. He watched the waves shove a log past. The way looked clear. He had about fifteen feet to get to the levee.

Daniel shoved his feet between rocks trying to get a firm grip. If he slipped, there was nothing to stop him from being swept away. Knees bent, he picked his way as fast as he could, gripping boulders, avoiding debris.

A fence post scraped his arm, but within minutes he'd reached the dry land.

"Daniel!"

Raven pointed at twelve o'clock. Trouble was headed his way. The wet dog clung to the log, but he stared at Daniel.

Daniel maneuvered himself in front of the log, and when the dog got close enough, Daniel grabbed him under his shoulders, falling backward.

Trouble's legs went out from under him. He whined and licked Daniel's face.

"You're welcome."

Daniel got up and studied the mountains. The clouds still hovered over the peak. He looked at his feet. The levee had narrowed. The water had already risen several inches. Within minutes the one rock jutting out of the wash would be underwater.

Desperate, he searched the churning rapids, then he saw Noah's dark hair. The man clung to a small rock, but his grip was slipping.

"Noah!"

He couldn't hear Daniel.

Noah's grip slipped, and he plunged under the water. Daniel gauged the distance, ready to jump in, but instead of heading toward the rock, the current carried him to the side.

"Damn it."

Daniel raced down the ten-foot rock. Noah was a few feet away. Daniel took a deep breath and plunged into the churning water. His hand gripped the collar of Noah's shirt. He grimaced at the weight.

Suddenly Noah's arm reached around and gripped Daniel's wrist. He heaved, dragging Noah to safety.

Trouble nosed Noah's hand, and the man rubbed the wet fur. "That was fun," he said, his voice full of irony. "Elijah?"

Daniel shook his head. "I don't know."

"There!" Raven yelled.

Daniel turned and recognized the man's sandy blond hair. Trouble let out a frantic bark.

"We can't reach him." Noah panted. "He's too far."

"But he can grab this." Daniel uncoiled the rope, forming a lasso. Who knew junior rodeo would come in handy in his life? He had one shot. He eyed the spot, swung the rope and let it fly. The loop landed just in front of Elijah.

If only he would see it. He looked very, very still.

Suddenly Elijah ducked underwater. A large log popped where his head had been. Then a strong tug grabbed the rope. He'd slipped his shoulder into it.

Daniel and Noah pulled on the line, veering the man toward their sinking island. He grabbed the rock and turned over, gasping for air.

"You guys always have this much fun on the job?" he gasped, coughing up some of the muddy water. "Remind me never to agree when you volunteer to pilot that flying gas can," he grumbled at Noah. "I'll take the lab any day of the week."

"Just another day at the office," Noah joked. "You make a good cowboy," he said to Daniel.

"We're not safe yet. The level's still rising." Water lapped at Daniel's feet.

Elijah couldn't hide his exhaustion.

"Can you make it?" Daniel asked Elijah. He gestured across the rapids.

Elijah nodded, his expression fierce and determined.

Daniel looped the rope around Trouble's collar, then each man secured the line between them. By the time they'd knotted themselves together, the level had reached their ankles. Trouble had become unsteady. He slipped down and nearly fell in.

"Ready?" Daniel asked.

They nodded. As quickly as possible, they maneuvered across the faster-moving flood. Finally, they reached the edge where Raven stood. Daniel sat back, his legs suddenly feeling the stress of being in thousands of square feet of roaring flood.

Raven dropped beside him and wrapped her arms

around him. "God, you scared me." She tentatively touched his cheek. "You're hurt."

"We're alive," he said.

"Barely. So let's not do that again." Noah scowled at Daniel. "You had to choose *this* godforsaken place to hide out during a flash flood?"

"It usually doesn't rain now. There's been a drought." He glanced at Raven. "We needed to be near town in case there was a breakthrough."

Noah's jaw throbbed. "How'd these guys find you?"

"I don't know. Not because they followed," Daniel said. "I made sure of it."

Elijah brushed some mud off his soaked jeans. "Maybe whoever's after Raven has a few toys. Satellite locators, listening devices."

Noah let out a curse. "I bet that's it. I gave the sheriff your coordinates because I needed to talk to you."

Raven looked stunned. "You don't think he's part of this?"

"I don't trust anyone right now," Daniel bit out, wiping his hand across his face. "If the sheriff's clean, then the perps probably bugged the phones. That would explain why they keep turning up." Daniel looked over at the raging water. "I wish we could get prints on the gunman. He handled that weapon like he's shot an automatic weapon before."

"You think he was military?" Noah asked.

"Yeah. Even hurt, the guy had a few moves." Daniel glanced down the wash. "I doubt we'll find his body anytime soon."

"What do we do now?" Raven asked, slipping her hand into Daniel's.

"Get out of here." He panned the landscape. "The second shooter could come back. I'll use the SAT phone to call the sheriff, pray his line's not being monitored. He'll have to arrange to pick us up. I can't get the four-wheel drive out for days." Daniel paused. "What were you guys doing out here anyway?"

"We couldn't get through to the SAT phone," Noah said. "Maybe the cave blocked the signal?"

"I didn't want to risk leaving it in the weather." Daniel cursed. "What was so important that you had to risk this weather? Not that I'm not damn glad you did."

Elijah met Noah's gaze, and the look they shared sent a chill of foreboding through Daniel. He tugged Raven up against him.

Her entire body tensed. "You know something, don't you?" What little color remained drained from her cheeks.

Elijah sucked in a deep breath. "I took the evidence we gathered and ran some preliminary tests. The blood on the toy box lid and the carpet was yours. So far I can't identify the other blood sample, but we're checking databases." He shifted. "I got curious about the hair from the locket so I tested it. The results are…surprising."

"Tell me," Raven pleaded.

"According to the DNA, the baby in the locket is not you, Raven. She's not your child, either. In fact, she's not related to you at all. But she is related to your attacker."

THE HOSPITAL LOOMED on the horizon. Christopher skid the dirt bike into the parking lot. He fought to pull the key out, then yanked off his helmet. They'd killed Tad. His only friend. The sole person who understood him.

The damn weapon Christopher had used had jammed. That bitch should be dead—her and the meddling men she'd somehow collected.

Just like a woman to ruin everything.

Christopher shoved the kickstand of his bike in place

and glared at the saddlebag where he had hid the weapon. He'd toss the thing later. A ballistics specialist could trace the bullets he'd managed to fire back to this gun. For now he had to figure out how to get rid of the woman. He had to fix this.

He stared up at the hospital. When his mother had called to tell him his sister was here, he couldn't believe it. She'd looked perfectly fine when he'd seen her. Rosy cheeks, healthy. Even better than the pictures he'd received while in Afghanistan. What had happened?

He didn't need this now. His mom could be so stupid and gullible. She'd been oblivious to his dad's lovers, his businesses, the illegals crossing their land for a fee. She wasn't capable of taking care of herself, so he was stuck with her.

He stomped into the hospital, mud clinging to his combat boots. His expression set, he ignored the fearful looks when he crossed the lobby to the elevator. Let them think what they liked. He hit the up button. The lit numbers above the doors crept down. Eight, seven…

Too slow. To hell with this. He stalked across the tiled floor and yanked the staircase door open. Then, taking two steps at a time, he rushed to the third floor and burst onto the pediatrics ward.

A nurse glared at him, then held her finger to her lips. He scowled at her, and she paled. Could she see her death in his eyes? He felt angry enough to kill anyone in his way.

Damn Tad. Why'd he have to get shot?

A floor-to-ceiling mural of giant bears with balloons grinned at him from the wall. He hated bears. If he had had his gun with him now, he would have strafed it.

He made his way down the hallway, looking for room three-fifteen. He stopped outside the oncology unit. Oncology couldn't be right. Three-fifteen was in the cancer ward? What the hell was wrong with Christina?

Bile rose in his throat, and he opened the door. His mother sat in a chair next to one of the room's cribs. Christopher looked down at the tuft of black hair and pale face of the baby in the crib.

"Who is this?"

His mother blinked through teary eyes. She kneaded her hands in her lap, refusing to meet his gaze. "I'm so, so sorry, Christopher. I wanted to tell you. Really I did, but she convinced me not to."

He stilled. "What are you talking about, Mother?"

His mother bit her lip. "This is Christina."

Christopher leaned over the pale, thin child lying so still. No. This wasn't right. "No way. Who's the other kid? Because this baby isn't Christina."

Pamela started crying.

"What's wrong with her?" He couldn't get over how sickly his adopted sister appeared, almost as if she were close to death.

Pamela choked back a sob. "She has aplastic anemia. Her body doesn't make enough new blood cells. It's like cancer."

"Can't they do something?"

"She has a severe case. Only a bone marrow transplant will cure her, and she has a rare blood type."

"Like me," he said. "But they do matches. We'll do a drive. We'll find a donor."

"I already did," Pamela said, pointing to the second crib in the room. "I found a perfect match."

Christopher looked at the second child, rosy cheeks, dark hair—the baby he'd thought was Christina. He stared at his mother, noting for the first time the intensity in her gaze, the almost manic energy. "Who is she?"

Pamela shook her head. "I promised I wouldn't tell you."

He whirled her around. "What's going on, Mother?"

Pamela stood over the sickly baby, looking down on her daughter with a tender smile, and stroked her cheek. "I missed you when you were in Afghanistan, honey. Despite everything you did and how you left, you were still my son." She turned to him. "I know I shouldn't say anything, but I've prayed about it. You have a right to know. I got a visit after you left the last time. From Chelsea."

Chelsea. "You hate her and never made it a secret," Christopher said, crossing his arms. "Why would she come to you?"

"She needed money," Pamela said, biting her lip, worry on her face.

Funny, his mother normally had a stoic expression that never revealed anything. It came from years of hiding her fear of her husband. Christopher had the same gift.

"Chelsea came to me with a…problem. You'd been forced into the military. She didn't have your number, and she was overwhelmed and embarrassed by her predicament." Pamela straightened. "I should never have agreed to keep it a secret, though. She lied to me the entire time. She's a whore, but as soon as I saw Christina, I knew—"

Pamela halted, as if terrified to go on.

Christopher could feel his brain revving with frustration, recognized the temper on the edge of an explosion. The army shrinks had tried to help him control himself. It usually worked when he wanted it to. He sucked in a breath while fighting against the urge to ram his fist through the wall. "Just *tell* me. What did you know?"

Pamela shrank away from him. "Stay calm, Christopher, please. Chelsea was pregnant. She never wanted you to know. Christina is *your* child. And my grandchild."

He clawed his scalp and let loose a loud string of curses.

Fighting against every violent instinct inside, he clutched the crib and stared down at the baby. *His* baby.

"She's mine?" He studied his daughter's features, so very familiar, then looked at the other baby. "She's a perfect bone marrow match? Weird. They even look alike. Or they would if Christina were well."

Pamela straightened. "That's because they're identical twins."

Christopher gasped. "And Chelsea didn't tell me?"

"You're not the only one Chelsea lied to," Pamela said. "These are your twin daughters, and Chelsea sold one of them to the highest bidder, to the woman on the television. I hurt her when I was trying to get your daughter back for you. I'm lucky I even found out what Chelsea did."

Christopher could feel his blood pressure mount. His temple throbbed; his hand shook. Fury like he'd never experienced erupted along his skin, raking like hot coals.

"Chelsea lied about everything," he snarled. "I would have loved her forever, and she betrayed me." He slipped a Bowie from his boot. "You don't have to worry about her anymore, Mother. She'll be dead by tonight."

"THE LITTLE GIRL in my locket is my attacker's baby?" Raven yelled.

This couldn't be happening. Her mind searched the snippets of memory she'd recovered, but she had nothing. "She's not mine?"

The horizon swayed.

Daniel scooped her into his arms before she hit the ground.

"Way to go, genius." He glared at Elijah, as he sat with Raven on the ground.

Raven clutched the locket around her neck. "There must be some mistake. I remember a pink blanket. I remember a baby. I've *had* a baby. The doctor said I delivered a child." Raven grasped Daniel's arm. "Why would I be wearing a locket of a baby that wasn't mine? It doesn't make sense. Who is she?"

Noah cleared his throat. "We're searching the DNA databases. It's taking a while to access the criminal and military records, but we may know part of the answer. Elijah, overachiever that he is, used age progression software to provide a guess of what the baby's parents might look like. We ran the image through my new facial recognition software. We found a 90 percent match to a woman from El Paso. We're trying to get her DNA."

Raven opened the locket, her heart twisting in grief. Over the past three days she'd come to love the baby's sweet smile, the sparkling eyes, the dimple. In her heart and mind she'd bonded with this baby. Raven's chest tightened in panic at the thought of losing her daughter, and she started hyperventilating. She grabbed her throat, trying to suck in air.

Daniel faced her. "Okay, darlin'. Bend over, take deep breaths. We'll figure this out."

She focused on calming her breathing. "You're saying my baby has *another* mother?"

This entire conversation felt wrong. It couldn't be true. And yet the nausea rising in Raven's gut was real. Some part of her believed Elijah and Noah were right.

Noah's expression softened. "We don't know everything yet," he offered.

"I'm sure there's an explanation," Elijah interrupted.

"A mug shot in El Paso matches the profile," Noah added. "The woman has moved since her arrest, though. They're tracking down the address. We'll know more after we interview her."

Daniel rubbed Raven's back, but she could barely feel

his touch. The image inside that locket had been the only touchstone in her life, besides Daniel, since she'd opened her eyes in that mine. Now she felt adrift.

"What's the possible mother's name?" Raven asked.

"Chelsea Rivera," Noah said. "She's got a string of arrests for shoplifting, a few minor drug charges, but nothing major."

Raven closed her eyes, willing her memory to explain the facts, but the name meant nothing to her. And her head had begun to throb once again.

She glanced at Daniel and could hardly stand to acknowledge the sympathy written on his face.

He hugged her closer. "We'll find out who the baby is. This could be a coincidence. Or perhaps you adopted this woman's baby."

"I wish I could remember."

Noah leaned forward. "Did the program work? Did you recall anything that will help?"

"Only that I might be married," Raven whispered.

Noah let out a low whistle. He met Daniel's gaze and raised a brow.

Raven ducked her head. What had happened between them was beautiful and special. She'd fallen for Daniel. She refused to believe that was wrong.

He turned Raven in his arms. "We *will* find the baby and the answers. I promise you that."

"Zane at CTC is running Chelsea's background, including finances," Elijah interjected. "If we get the woman's blood sample, we'll be able to confirm or disprove her identity."

"We have to talk to her. She might be able to clear everything up," Daniel said, standing, helping Raven to her feet. "We might be mere hours away from answers."

"I pray so." Raven chewed on her lower lip. "But I'm terrified I won't like the answers."

The sound of another helicopter broke through her thoughts. A rescue chopper this time.

"I'll get our supplies from the cave," Daniel said to Noah and Elijah. "You all grab the sheriff's attention."

Raven slipped her hand into Daniel's. "I'll help you," she said quietly, her fingers trembling.

He didn't argue.

Trouble followed them into the cave, close to Raven's side.

"You okay?" Daniel asked.

"Not even close," she said. "How can this be? I remember a wedding. I remember a baby who may or may not be mine. I may have adopted a child. Why would any of these things make someone want me dead? Did I steal the baby?"

Daniel brought her face within two inches of his own. "Don't be crazy. We'll figure it out."

She nodded her head and climbed up the rocks to their cave.

Standing next to him, she stared inside the rock haven, the place they'd made love, the place she'd felt so close to Daniel. She glanced over at him. "I was happy here for a few hours. At peace, if that makes sense."

"Me, too. For the first time in a long time." He bent his head and touched her lips lightly with his. "I don't regret holding you in my arms, Raven. No matter what happens, I won't ever be sorry I made love to you."

He knelt down and started stuffing items in the duffel while Raven gathered up the baby toys and packed Noah's small bag.

They were done too quickly. "I want to disappear," she said. "I don't want to be part of this craziness anymore. Does that make me a coward?"

"It makes you human," he said.

Daniel hitched the pack on his shoulder and led the way out of the cave. Raven paused for a moment. The water had slowed some, but still churned violently. She shivered, remembered dangling from the side until Daniel had rescued her. They both could have died.

The limbs on the cracked trunk they'd climbed on swayed, catching her attention. The whip was still tied to the tree and hung against the bark. She stepped toward it, and Daniel stopped her.

"I don't want it, Raven. I don't need it anymore. It's just a memory now. Not a demon."

Daniel held out his hand to her. Raven had to look back once. How ironic. Daniel had abandoned his memory on the edge of a cliff in the middle of nowhere, while she'd spent three days praying to remember.

Now all she wanted was to forget the past few hours ever happened and find her baby.

DANIEL COULDN'T SIT still. He paced in front of the window in the sheriff's office after eliminating the listening device planted on the outside phone line. Their only good news was that Lucy and Hondo had both come through surgery. While it might be a long recovery, particularly for the small woman, they would survive.

Noah and Elijah had left to trace the dead shooter's motorcycle that had been left at the top of the mesa. They'd come back with a stolen vehicle report, no leads and no prints other than the owner's. The guy must have used gloves.

Another fruitless path. Man, they needed a break.

Raven sat stiff in the wooden chair across from the sheriff's desk, her entire body tense and wired.

The sheriff tilted his Stetson back. “Raven, you *still* don’t remember anything?”

Daniel crossed his arms in irritation. “She already told you she didn’t, Galloway. Just let her alone.”

“It’s okay,” Raven said with gratitude in her eyes. “He has to ask, and I wish I had answers.” She turned to the sheriff. “I see flashes of scenes, but it’s only bits and pieces. A wedding, a pink blanket. Nothing that helps. Certainly nothing about Chelsea Rivera. But I won’t give up. I have to remember. I don’t have a choice.”

Damn, she was grace under pressure. Daniel couldn’t help but admire her. She might have been thrown by the news that the baby in the locket wasn’t hers, but she’d rallied, hounding Noah and Elijah for every detail they had. Unfortunately there was nothing more.

The fax machine in the corner whirred to life.

Raven jumped to her feet, and Galloway strode to the machine. He perused the message.

“Well?” she asked. “Is there any news for us?”

“The name Wayne Harrison mean anything to you?” the sheriff asked.

She rubbed her temple, rolling the name through her mind. “No. Maybe. I don’t know,” she said. “I feel like I *should* know it. This is *so* frustrating.”

“Who is he?” Daniel asked.

“According to CTC, a draft was drawn on an account jointly held by Wayne Harrison and his wife, Olivia. It was made out to C.R.—Chelsea Rivera—for over fifty thousand dollars about twenty-one months ago.

“Even more interesting than the amount is the fact that within a few months of receiving the money, Ms. Rivera entered the hospital.” The sheriff handed Daniel the fax. “On the maternity ward.”

"And my baby might be hers?" Raven gulped. "Are you saying I might be this Olivia Harrison?"

"I don't know, but Chelsea's hospital bill was also paid by Wayne and Olivia Harrison. Could be a private adoption. Could be something else."

Sheriff Galloway stroked his chin. "No birth certificate, though. Kind of weird. And I don't believe in odd coincidences. Money for a baby doesn't usually result in a legal transaction."

Raven glanced from one man to the other and fell back in her seat. "Oh, God. Do you think the baby was bought on the black market?"

Daniel recognized the moment she understood the possibility. Her eyes widened, then she shook her head. "No. I wouldn't do such a thing. I wouldn't buy a child. I can't be this Olivia Harrison."

He knelt in front of her. "Don't jump to conclusions. The woman I know would need facts first."

Raven's hands shook, and her fingers had gone cold. "But do we even know who I am, what I was capable of before they left me for dead?" She rubbed her temple. "It doesn't matter." She opened the locket and held it up. "This baby exists. Who I am doesn't matter right now. She's out there somewhere, and I need to find her. I won't stop until I know for sure that she's safe and loved. Whether she's mine or not, we have to help her."

Noah burst through the sheriff's door. "We have a maternal DNA match," he said. "Chelsea Rivera was a witness in a felony. They did a DNA profile before they eliminated her as a suspect."

"How did you—" Sheriff Galloway started.

"Don't ask," Noah muttered. "The point is the preliminary results are a match. Chelsea Rivera is that baby's mother. And we have her address. She lives in El Paso, not two hours from here."

"Then there's only one thing to do," Daniel said. "We visit Chelsea Rivera and find out what she knows about the baby in the locket."

Chapter Ten

The midafternoon sun glared down on the loaner SUV's windshield, and Daniel cursed the fact that he had no sunglasses. The temperature had to be creeping up on eighty degrees. Trouble sat in the backseat panting. Fall hadn't hit El Paso yet, but then, most things in Texas were ornery like that.

Daniel let out a slow breath when they drove by Chelsea Rivera's current address. The house had been easy enough to find.

"Quiet neighborhood," Noah commented. "Run-down, but not a war zone."

"I'll circle the block." Daniel kept the speed steady, as if they had a destination in mind. "We'll find a secure location to park the car."

He took a quick pass around the block, eyeing potential escape routes.

"How about there?" Raven asked when they came upon an alley.

Cinder-block walls provided cover, and Daniel nodded.

"Good eye," Noah said. "Only a few houses down."

Daniel backed the SUV into the narrow space between two houses and set the vehicle to Park. With Trouble not far behind, Raven climbed out of the backseat, while Daniel opened his door and Noah followed. They stood just out of sight of Chelsea's house, but Daniel's nerves were frayed and edgy.

"Seems quiet," Noah said. "I doubt we'll need backup. Galloway and Elijah can let us know how the Harrison lead pans out, and we may solve this thing before dinner. I know this great cantina—"

Daniel raised his hand. "Don't go there. Every time the situation seems real quiet, Raven and I have almost gotten killed," Daniel said. "Noah, stay with her. I'll signal you."

"What?" Raven said. "You think you're going to just walk up to this woman's door, and she'll talk to you? I hate to tell you this, but you're big, muscular and intimidating, and you walk enough like a cop that she's going to be wary. I should go, too."

"Not happening." His gaze fell to her necklace. "Can I borrow the locket?" he asked.

Raven set her jaw, but she lifted the chain over her head. "You are the most stubborn man." He could see her desire to run across the street and question Chelsea herself, no matter the danger.

Sometimes Raven had a backbone of steel. Usually something that completely turned him on. Not right now, though. He'd gone cold with worry. He had to keep her safe, but whoever wanted her dead seemed two steps ahead of them all the time. The thought wasn't comforting.

Wary of a trap, Daniel worked his way two houses down, keeping out of sight as much as possible. Across from the target location, he paused behind a hedge and hunkered down. He glanced over his shoulder. Noah, Raven and Trouble remained hidden from view, unless you knew where to look. Daniel knew she'd be safe. Noah wouldn't hesitate to sacrifice himself for her.

Neither would Daniel.

He remembered the look he and Noah had exchanged

earlier. They understood each other. If anything happened, Noah would get Raven to CTC headquarters in Carder; then he'd come back and finish what Daniel had started.

He stepped onto the pavement, out of the direct line of sight of the front door and window, then crossed the pothole-littered street. The neighborhood was probably last on the list to get any work done. Not enough registered voters on this street to pressure the city council.

A quick glance in the backyard revealed nothing but a sad thatch of grass and a few struggling perennials in a small planter. He signaled Noah to keep alert, then walked up the broken sidewalk. Once there, he stood just to the right of the doorknob.

The neighborhood was silent. No curtains moving. This was one of those revolving rental streets where neighbors just didn't want to get involved with people who might not be around the next month. Isolation was a lot safer.

Daniel didn't like standing here in the open. His Spidey-sense was working overtime, though he had nothing to base it on. Daniel's shoulders tensed; the hair on the back of his neck stood at attention.

He shifted his shoulder and tucked his Glock within easy reach. He knocked on the door.

A wooden creak sounded through the poorly insulated walls. The curtain quivered.

"Ma'am. I know you're in there. My name is Daniel Adams. I just need to ask a few questions. It's about your baby."

"Go away. Please," a frightened voice begged.

"Not until I talk to you."

"Who…who are you?" she asked, obviously terrified. "Who sent you?"

"No one." Daniel held up the locket to the window. "I'm hoping you can tell me about this child."

The curtains pulled back, and a dark-haired woman with terrified eyes blinked at him. Her cheek was discolored, as if someone had hit her. Daniel's gut burned.

"Do you need help, Chelsea?" he asked softly.

"No, I need you to—" Her gaze honed in on the locket like a laser beam. "Where'd you get that? Mrs. H would never have given it away."

"This locket belongs to Mrs. H?"

"Yes." The woman's hand moved to her throat and lifted a gold heart from beneath her blouse. "She gave me one just like it. To remember."

A soft smile crossed Chelsea's face.

The sound of wood splintering toward the back of the house was followed by a scream. Gunfire exploded, then glass shattered the window where she stood.

Daniel heard a dull thud hit the floor.

He gripped his Glock and shoved his shoulder into the door. The jamb gave way. Chelsea Rivera lay on the floor, her face gone, blood streaming from a horrifying head wound. The bullet had entered from the back and exploded.

The back door slammed.

Knowing Raven was safe with Noah, Daniel raced through the house to the kitchen and out a side door.

Nearby, a motorcycle revved and the powerful engine roared. The shooter headed west. Daniel ran into the front yard, then into the street, his boots thudding on the pavement. The roar of the motor grew louder. Bike tires squealed. Daniel leaped toward the sound, hoping to get a glimpse of the plate.

He caught sight of a black Harley racing down the street, its license plate covered with mud and unreadable, just like the sedan from the drive-by shooting. The guy wore leathers and a very expensive helmet.

The shooter was definitely not from this neighborhood. He was rich. Panting, Daniel watched the bike speed away.

He slipped the gun into the waist of his jeans and jogged back to Noah and Raven.

She stood behind the SUV and peered around Noah, who'd placed himself between her and danger.

"You see anything useful?" Daniel asked.

Noah shook his head. "Sorry. Too far away."

Raven looked up at Daniel. "What happened?"

"Chelsea was shot right after I got there. She didn't say much, but she had a locket just like yours."

"She did?" Raven asked, her expression tentative. "Are you saying he killed her?"

Daniel nodded. "She didn't make it. I'm sorry."

He dropped the gold heart into her palm. "But Chelsea said the woman who gave her the locket had an identical necklace."

Raven stilled. "You know who I am?"

"Mrs. Harrison gave Chelsea that locket." Daniel said softly. "I think we finally know your name."

SIRENS RAGED ALL around the SUV when Daniel pulled out of the alley. Raven's heartbeat quickened, and her fingers gripped the scrub pants she wore. She held her breath when Daniel slowed and moved to the right. Three speeding police cars passed the SUV with lights flashing, but the cops just swerved into Chelsea's driveway.

"Will Noah be okay?" she asked. "What if they arrest him?"

"He can handle himself. Noah has connections. Even if they do arrest him, he'll be out in a matter of minutes," Daniel said. "It's more important that we find Wayne Harrison fast. I don't want to stay here to explain what we were doing visiting Chelsea, or why you're wearing an identical locket to hers."

"They'd never believe what's happened to me," Raven said. "If *I* heard my story, *I'd* think it was a lie."

"Amnesia's hard to believe, since you can't answer most of their questions. *If* you're Mrs. Harrison, then you paid Chelsea. Fifty thousand dollars changed hands. There's no baby and no birth certificate. Very suspicious."

"And I can't tell them why any of it happened." Raven rubbed her forehead, trying to ease the headache that had returned. "What a nightmare."

"For now Noah will have to handle the questioning. Hopefully Wayne Harrison will have enough information for us to explain your presence in Chelsea's life."

She touched the cut on the side of her forehead. "Do you think whoever killed Chelsea is the man who attacked me?"

"It's a safe bet." An edge tinged Daniel's voice. "I'm looking forward to shaking some answers out of your—" He stopped. "Out of Wayne Harrison."

Her husband. That's what he'd meant to say.

She drank in Daniel's strong profile, his hands, his fingers that had caressed her, touched her, loved her. She didn't want to remember giving herself to anyone but Daniel. Raven scratched the base of the ring finger of her left hand and voiced her greatest fear. "Do you really think he's my husband?"

"No. I think you *were* married," Daniel said. "Your dreams have been accurate as far as we know. There *is* a baby. And Wayne Harrison is our only lead." Daniel slid her a heated glance. "I don't want you to be married, Raven. I want what I can't have."

Before she could ask what he meant, his phone rang and he pressed Speaker. "Adams here."

"It's Elijah. We got a hit on Raven. I'm messaging you the info and a photo."

A quick pull of the turn signal, and Daniel stopped by the side of the road and put the SUV into Park.

Raven turned toward Daniel, praying and dreading the scan would have all the answers.

A tone sounded. Daniel tapped the message, and Raven held her breath.

A newspaper article appeared as an image on the phone's screen.

Oh, God. A wedding announcement.

One glance at the photo and caption made Raven gasp.

Mr. and Mrs. Wayne and Olivia Harrison.

"It's me," she said sadly. "Me and the man from my dream."

PAMELA WINTER STARED at the small baby in the hospital's crib, hoping for a miracle. She couldn't remember the last time she'd slept. Grit stung her eyes each time she blinked.

Her baby girl looked so pale.

"You'll be okay, Christina." Pamela caressed the thinning hair on her beautiful daughter. "We have to disappear, but you'll get the bone marrow transplant, and everything will be better."

With care, Pamela lifted Christina out of the crib and sat with her in the rocking chair. The little girl in the adjacent crib whined, staring up at them. She held out her arms.

Pamela ignored the healthy baby. She'd have to entertain herself until Christina was well. And she would be well. Pamela had chosen their new safe house carefully. Near the Mayo Clinic. She'd hidden enough money from Christopher that she wouldn't have to work again. With Christina's sister as the donor, things should move fast at the new hospital. Everything was going to work.

All she had to do now was trigger Christopher's temper enough so he'd hang himself, and then she and her daughters would disappear. Forever.

"I'll make you all better," she whispered in Christina's ear. "He will never hurt you."

Heavy footsteps paused at the door. Pamela stilled, afraid to look around. It shouldn't be Christopher. After the lies she'd told him, surely he'd left to kill Chelsea for her. Pamela was too busy to do it herself.

The pediatric hematologist came up beside her.

She looked up and took in his solemn expression. "What's wrong?"

Panic twisted her gut, just like the day she'd learned of Christina's illness. During the horrifying search for a matching donor, Pamela had finally discovered the doctor who had revealed Chelsea had had twins. After that, it had been easy to find the other baby. The Harrisons hadn't hidden their adoption.

Pamela had thought her troubles were ending. How wrong she'd been.

The doctor frowned. "Christina's blood work doesn't look good. Since her sister is a match, we need to start the chemotherapy right away. Otherwise, if Christina's health deteriorates, it might be too late."

Pamela froze in the rocker. Time was up. She'd have to eliminate the final risks.

The forger was gone; Chelsea was gone.

All that remained were Wayne and Olivia Harrison.

And one other.

The only other.

Christopher.

She wrung her hands. Could she kill her own son? Did she have the nerve?

The baby whimpered and rolled over. She opened her beautiful eyes, dull and weak with fatigue.

Pamela melted at the sight and hugged her daughter close. She couldn't lose her. She met the doctor's gaze. "May I stay with her 24/7?"

"I'll set things up for that and the chemo," he said, and left the room.

"And by the time you do all that, we'll be gone," Pamela whispered, humming. "Mama will do anything for you, baby girl. Anything." She rose and placed her precious bundle in the crib.

"We'll leave here soon, baby. Very soon."

Ashes, ashes, we all fall down.

DANIEL STARED OUT the SUV window at the late-afternoon sun, hating Elijah for the news he was giving over the phone.

Trouble had found himself a cool spot in the cargo area of the vehicle. He'd been too quiet. Maybe the mutt sensed the high level of emotions.

"I'm married?" Raven whispered, obviously devastated. "No. It can't be."

"You're not married now," Elijah rushed to say. "You were. You and your husband divorced shortly after you adopted your daughter."

The words swirled in Daniel's head. Raven wasn't married. She'd adopted a daughter, but she wasn't married anymore.

"What's my daughter's name? Please, Elijah. Tell me you know her name," Raven pleaded.

"Hope," Elijah said, clearing his throat. "The baby's name is Hope."

Raven's face lit up in a smile. Daniel had never seen such an expression of joy on her face.

She threw her arms around his neck and hugged him. “She’s real, Daniel.” Raven buried her face in his shirt, her choking sobs unstoppable. “She’s real. Hope’s mine. She’s my baby.”

“Yes, darlin’, she’s yours.” Daniel set Raven back and wiped her tears away with his thumb.

“But where is she?” Raven asked.

“Elijah?” Daniel prompted, praying there was more good news, but when silence settled over the phone, he grimaced. “Can you tell us anything else?”

The forensics expert cleared his throat. “Raven has full custody, no visitation for the ex-husband, Wayne, and there’s no nanny, but, I’m sorry, Rav…Olivia, I don’t know where Hope is.”

“I have to find her. And, Elijah, call me Raven,” she said softly, wrapping her arms around herself. “I don’t know how I feel about this Olivia Harrison yet.”

Daniel hugged her close, and she collapsed against his chest, the pressure of the past few days finally taking its toll. He wanted to promise her the world, but despite the progress he’d made, his demons could coming roaring back anytime. So he’d conquered the sound of a whip. His other issues would be much harder.

Daniel faced the fact that he might not be there for her forever, but he could find Raven’s daughter. He ignored how his throat had closed off at the idea of letting Raven go. He shoved the regret from his mind. “Run a check on Wayne Harrison. I want to know if he owns a motorcycle, a Harley in particular, *and* if he has any connection to the mines surrounding Trouble, Texas.”

“Will do,” Elijah said. “We’ll get back to you with the information and his address.”

He signed off, and Raven took a few deep breaths. “You think my husband did this?”

Daniel shrugged. “It’s a strong possibility. Most of the time when a child disappears, a family member is responsible. He never reported you missing. That could mean he didn’t want your absence noticed.”

“No one reported me. Don’t I have *any* friends or relatives? Was I all alone?”

Daniel couldn’t stop himself from touching her in an attempt to comfort her, to keep the possibilities from tearing apart her hope. With each caress she leaned into him more, and something deep within him shifted as he eased closer. How would he live without her?

“Why would he take the baby?” she asked, her voice etched with pain.

“Maybe he changed his mind. Maybe he regretted giving her up. I could never give up my daughter unless… unless I was a danger to her well-being.”

She fisted the material of his shirt. “You’d never hurt someone you love.”

He appreciated her faith, but it was misplaced. “My father had flashbacks like I do. He ruined my sisters’ lives. He hurt them badly.”

“He hurt you, too.” She tightened her grip. “How did you cope with his death?”

Daniel wrapped his arms around her. “I became the man of the family after he killed himself. I did what I had to do.” He tilted her head to him and stared at her lips. They parted, inviting him to lose himself in her. But he knew Raven being with him would ultimately break her heart. Not to mention his own.

Thankfully his phone trilled again. He pressed Speaker. “Adams.”

“Olivia?” a man’s questioning voice filtered into the truck. “I’m looking for Olivia Harrison. I was told I could reach her at this number.”

Daniel squeezed the phone until his knuckles whitened. Who the hell was giving out his private line? "Who are you?"

"Wayne Harrison."

Raven bit her lip. "Wayne?"

"Yeah. You sound strange. Are you all right?"

Even though Daniel didn't know her ex, and Wayne's words were all fine, his voice was off. Very hesitant and cautious. Something was wrong.

Daniel scowled. Or else Daniel just hated the guy on principle. What kind of jerk would give up his daughter—or Raven?

She finally answered. "I'm fine..."

"Then where have you been? I've been worried. I called your house a half-dozen times." Wayne's voice broke. "I mean, I know I'm your ex, but even then—" He sounded sincere, like he really cared that she'd been missing. Daniel would give him that.

According to the article on both Olivia and her ex that Elijah had sent to Daniel's phone, the guy was an accountant with an Ivy League education, and he made a good living. Why wouldn't someone smart like Olivia want to be with someone like Wayne Harrison? They made a perfect couple. Steady, reliable.

"Umm...why were you trying to reach me?"

Wayne paused. "Look, this guy called me asking about your daughter. I told him I'd signed over full custody and don't have anything to do with her, but he doesn't believe me. He claims he's her birth father. I thought you said the woman we paid had full rights. Did you make that up?"

"Are you saying you don't have the baby?" Raven asked softly.

"Why would you ask me that?" Wayne asked, his voice

low. "Of course I don't have her. What's wrong with you, Olivia?"

Raven bowed her head. If her ex didn't have Hope, then they were back to square one—except they knew her name.

"What was the birth father's name?" she asked, taking her cue from Daniel.

"He didn't tell me. Look," Wayne said, "let me come over right now, and we can talk about this. I don't… I'm concerned. You sound really weird."

Daniel shook his head, and Raven tipped her head in agreement. "I can't. There are things happening…"

"Fine. I get it," Wayne interrupted. "I know I let you down when I didn't want to raise someone else's kid. I thought I could do it, so sue me. But, Olivia, we can still be friends."

"I don't know," Raven answered.

Wayne's voice dropped to nearly a whisper. "We need to talk. This guy. He's—" Wayne grunted. "Dangerous. If I can't come to you, then come my way. I'm at the El Paso house."

She bit her lip and sent Daniel a questioning look. He debated. Wayne could be telling the truth. Maybe, just maybe, they'd get a lead. Daniel nodded his agreement, and simultaneously sent out a text to Elijah and Noah to track down more information.

"I'll be there," she said.

"Soon?" Wayne urged. "Could you come now?"

"As soon as I can," she promised.

Daniel ended the call, then punched in Elijah's and Noah's numbers for a three-way conversation. When they were on the line, Daniel let the temper he'd been holding flare. "Which one of you boneheads gave Wayne Harrison my cell number?"

"I did." Elijah's voice was matter-of-fact, calm and non-apologetic. "Sheriff Galloway contacted him during our investigation. The guy called back, said he needed to talk to his wife. From GPS I got his location. Figured we wanted to have a conversation with him one way or another. He still a suspect?"

Daniel rubbed the back of his neck where a tension headache had started moving up his skull. Elijah was right, damn him. Daniel glanced at Raven. He was emotionally involved. He couldn't deny it, and it was affecting his judgment.

"The conversation was odd," Daniel said, clutching the phone tighter, "but I don't think he has the baby. He does have answers, but he's evasive."

"Then we go to him," Noah said.

The options kept narrowing, particularly without a birth certificate. Daniel knew they were missing a piece, something critical, something important. Something that would reveal who wanted Raven dead and who had taken her child. If it wasn't Wayne, then who? And why? There had to be a reason.

Daniel just prayed that when he figured out the truth, it wouldn't be too late.

CHRISTOPHER SHOVED THE gun into Wayne Harrison's temple. "Well done. Guess this shows you why you shouldn't leave your back door unlocked. You never know who will just walk in off the streets."

Wayne dropped the phone back on the cradle. "Please. Take anything you want, just let me go. I did what you asked. I don't know anything."

"Shut up before you piss me off. Do you have a basement?" Christopher asked.

"W-why? What are you going to do to me?" Wayne's voice shook.

"Not very brave, are you? What, you think I'm going to kill you down there, bury your body like some deranged serial killer?" Christopher chuckled. "Might be a change of pace, but I'm on a mission, my friend. A very important mission."

Christopher dragged the gun's barrel across Wayne's cheek. "You paid fifty thousand bucks for my kid, didn't you?"

"I didn't want to," Wayne protested. "It was all Olivia. She met the mother at the ob-gyn, and the woman said she couldn't take care of her baby. When Olivia lost our baby, she got in touch with her. That's all I know."

Christopher twisted around to backhand the coward. "What was the mother's name?"

Wayne rubbed the blood from his lip, his eyes wide and wary.

Christopher again pushed the gun to Wayne's head. "Her name, or you're dead."

"Chelsea Rivera." The words rushed out.

"You're dead. You know too much."

"Please," Wayne begged. "I don't know who you are. I won't tell anyone. I swear."

Christopher kicked the man in the groin. Wayne collapsed, and Christopher shoved him over onto his back. "Men like you disgust me. My father chewed people like you up and spit them out his entire career. My mother was right. We end this here. Today. My daughters will be with me from now on."

He pressed his boot into Wayne's windpipe. The guy turned red and sucked in short breaths. "Now, where's the basement?"

Gasping for air, Wayne pointed to a door just across the living room.

"Crawl," Christopher ordered. "Belly crawl like the sniveling worm you are."

Wayne made his way slowly to the door and opened it. A narrow staircase disappeared into the dark.

Christopher smiled, checking the layout. Perfect. One exit. One entrance. Like shooting targets during boot camp. Tad would've had fun with this one. A small twinge of regret nipped at Christopher's conscience. Tad had been a good friend. He shouldn't have died like that. The man watching over Raven would pay. Christopher would take his time finishing off that one.

"Get up and turn on the light, Harrison."

Wayne rose and flipped the switch.

"Down the stairs."

Suddenly Wayne whirled around and shoved his shoulder into Christopher's chest. He stumbled back.

"Idiot." Christopher raised his gun and fired a gut shot. Harrison was dead. He just didn't know it yet.

Blood seeped through his shirt. Wayne groaned and grabbed at the wound. "You're crazy!"

Christopher shook his head. "My dad taught me how to shoot. Uncle Sam taught me how to kill." He grabbed Harrison's hair and gazed into the coward's fearful eyes. "Now get down there. I'm not through with you yet."

Chapter Eleven

Raven didn't think Daniel could drive any faster. He whizzed around the curves like an Indy driver. She peered into the afternoon sun and eyed a street sign for North Mesa. If Trouble didn't have dog ears, she might just scream. Instead she clenched her fist, her nails biting into her palm.

"Not familiar?" Daniel asked.

"Not a glimmer, and I'm starting to wonder if I'll ever remember."

"It's only been a few days. You're still healing." He set his hand next to hers on the seat. "Even if you don't, you'll go on. You'll create a new life. You and your daughter—when we find her."

Her heart fluttered at the nearness of his hand. But he didn't hold it. Was he trying to tell her something? To pull away? Her heart stuttered a bit, because in her mind, she could see a picture as clearly as the landscape through this upscale neighborhood. Daniel, her, Hope. A life together. She would be his. *If* he wanted her.

She couldn't call it love, because she had no frame of reference, but if love meant your heart skipped whenever he whispered your name, if love meant trusting a man with *your* life, with your child's life, if love meant having complete faith a man would always think of you before he thought of himself, if love meant knowing a man could be counted on to protect you heart and soul, then she had to believe she loved Daniel.

She clutched at her shirt just above her heart and took a shuddering breath. My God. She loved him. Suddenly she couldn't think; her leg bounced and she tried to focus, watching his hands steer, his eyes study the surroundings and his small smile when he met her gaze.

He pulled up to a large two-story house, the white stucco gleaming and the red tile contrasting, and stopped. "Your ex has a nice place," he said, lowering the windows a bit and opening the door.

Trouble started barking frantically, turning on the seat.

"Trouble. Stay," he said. The dog jumped into the backseat and stuck his nose out the window. "Don't worry, I'll leave the air-conditioning on for you, but this isn't the kind of neighborhood you can roam free in." He glanced around. The place oozed upper middle class. "I don't want to bail you out of the dog pound."

Raven unlocked her car door but stopped when Daniel's phone rang. He glanced down and hit Speaker. "How close are you?"

"Not too far," Noah said. He paused for a second. "Do you want the scoop on Olivia Harrison?"

Raven's back tensed. She bit her lip. Did she want to know? What if—?

Coward. They needed whatever would help them find the baby. She didn't matter. Her daughter did. She sent Daniel a quick nod.

"Give us what's relevant."

"Raven, honey? You okay with that?" Noah said softly.

"I need to know," she said, her voice barely loud enough to be heard.

"Well, you got a few facts from that bio in the wedding announcement, but you caught yourself a smart one, Daniel. Try to let some rub off on you. Olivia graduated magna cum laude in biochemistry. Figured out something about DNA sequencing that I can't understand. She's got several patents that brought in a boatload of money. That house you're standing in front of? Her ex got it in the divorce settlement."

"I'm not surprised she's smart," Daniel said. "When she started spouting off chemical formulas on day one, I knew she was something special."

Raven's cheeks heated, and she squirmed in her seat.

Noah cleared his throat. "I did find out one thing. Brace yourself, honey. You weren't wrong about having a baby. Two years ago you were pregnant. Seven months along. Something went wrong, and your baby daughter was stillborn. I'm *so* sorry."

Raven's heart started pounding. She doubled over and grabbed her belly. She could almost feel the pain gripping her stomach. Hard contractions, without hope. Flashes burned into her mind. Despair so deep she could barely breathe.

Daniel grabbed her and wrapped his arms around her, holding her tight against him. His warm breath whispered against her ear. "Listen to my voice, Raven. Don't let it take over. Come back to me."

Tears wet her eyelashes. She glanced up at him. "My baby is dead," she said.

"Yes. You named her Sarah," Noah said. "A few months later you adopted a baby girl. Chelsea Rivera was the birth mother. That fifty thousand dollars paid her expenses. About a month after the adoption was final, your husband filed for divorce."

"Jerk," Daniel muttered.

"Hope," Raven whispered, begging her mind to remember the baby's face, not from a photo, but from a memory. She opened the locket and stared at the dark-haired baby. "How old is she now?" Raven asked.

"Eighteen months."

Raven leaned against Daniel, soaking in his strength. She needed to find Hope. He rubbed her back for a moment. Finally she straightened. "Wayne Harrison said the baby's birth father wants her. Who is the father?"

"I'll keep looking. I found your pediatrician's records—don't ask how—but I can't seem to locate her birth certificate. I'm hoping Elijah can unravel the state vital statistics records."

Daniel glanced at his watch. "How far from Harrison's house are you?" he asked.

"Another half hour," Noah said.

"We're going in. Maybe we can get a description of the father from Wayne, see if he matches the jumper in the canyon. Or if he was riding a motorcycle."

"Watch your back. Elijah and I will be there as soon as we can."

Daniel stuffed his phone into his pocket and looked down at Raven. He slid his thumb under her eye and cupped her cheek. "You up for this?"

"I don't know him," she said softly. "I have nothing invested in Wayne Harrison. Hope is all I care about." Raven gripped the locket. "We have to find her. This man—whoever he is—can't have her."

"He won't get her. She belongs with you."

Raven nodded, but Daniel's words tugged at a huge fear. "If I never remember, can I be her mother? Will they take her away?"

"No way. You are passionate, determined and loving. From the moment I found you, all you've thought about is finding that little girl. You believed when everyone else doubted. That's what a mother is. Believe me, I know. I have a good one." He tucked a strand of her black hair behind her ear. "If they do question your parenting ability, I have a lot of friends in very high places."

Raven hugged him and kissed his cheek. "Let's find my daughter, Daniel."

"Let's meet the ex," Daniel groused, his eyes dark. "I still think he's a jerk for abandoning you."

"We don't know why," Raven said.

"I don't care. Any man who would abandon his child doesn't deserve sympathy."

She winced, knowing he was talking about *his* father, *his* family as much as Wayne Harrison. Together they headed down a long sidewalk to the front door. The manicured lawn was perfect. The plants and trees were perfect. Nothing looked out of place; it was as if the house belonged on the cover of a magazine.

"Not real lived-in, huh?" Daniel said.

"Sterile," Raven muttered. "I can't believe I lived here."

Daniel rang the bell. After a few moments, he knocked on the door.

"That's odd. He knew we were coming."

His posture changed. Raven recognized the awareness. She'd seen him in this stance, as if searching for danger by sight, smell and feel. He glanced around the neighborhood. "Nothing unusual." He peered in the front window. "The house looks deserted, but then again, it could be he's the ultimate anal neat freak."

"I wish I knew," Raven said. "Is Noah sure this is the right house?"

"Noah doesn't make mistakes like that, but I'll double-check." A quick text later, Daniel pressed the doorbell a second time. "This is it."

He tried the knob. It opened.

"Maybe something happened to him..."

"Mr. Harrison?" he called. "Wayne?"

"Basement," a pained voice said. "I...fell."

They rushed to an open door. Daniel flipped the light switch, but the stairwell remained dark.

"Wayne?" Raven called.

"Here," a muffled voice muttered. "I need help. I can't walk."

Daniel pulled out the small but powerful flashlight from his pocket. Raven gave him a look. He shrugged. "It's come in handy."

Daniel led the way down the tunnellike stairs, shining the light on the steep steps. She didn't want to fall. One head injury a week was plenty.

A sniffle sounded from across the room. Daniel turned at the landing, then stilled.

"Run," he hissed at her, blocking her view.

"If you want to see my daughter again, Olivia, you'll join us," a soft, threatening voice promised.

DANIEL COULDN'T BELIEVE he'd let them get into this position. Trouble had warned him. Without hesitation, Raven stepped around him and down the last couple of steps. Inside he wanted to scream at her to run, but she wouldn't. He couldn't expect her to. This guy had played the only card that would trump her own safety. Hope.

Just as Daniel wouldn't hesitate to risk his life for Raven.

He scanned the area. Two closed doors on one wall. A bathroom, maybe, and a storage closet, though what Wayne had in a room with a steel door made Daniel wonder. As to exits, several high windows lined the top of the wall, but Noah wouldn't be able to see in with the darkening blinds. The rest of the basement was a typical man cave, with video games, a big-screen television, comfortable sofas and recliners, and a bar and refrigerator.

All in all, they were stuck in another freakin' cave. He and Raven couldn't get away from them. Of course, this time they had company.

RAVEN'S EX SAT bound to a chair, his entire body stiff, his fear palpable. His face had been battered; blood stained his side, dripping down to the floor. The man's pasty complexion made Daniel curse. The guy was still losing blood. He could go into shock at any moment.

Daniel shifted, trying to ease his hand to his pocket. If he could warn Noah, or maybe reach his Glock—

"I wouldn't do that," his captor said. "I won more than my share of shooting awards in boot camp. Phone and gun on the floor. Slide them to me."

Well, hell. The guy had training. Knowing he had to take the risk, Daniel flicked the edge of the phone, sending a warning signal to Noah, then he did as instructed.

"I bet you carry a knife, too."

Daniel weighed the alternatives.

"Don't get cute with me, spook. I find you lied, I won't hesitate to kill her. That's my plan anyway."

Knowing he couldn't risk Raven's life, Daniel slipped the Bowie from his ankle sheath and tossed it on the ground. The knife didn't make any noise on the carpet.

Raven stepped forward. "Where's Hope? Let me see her."

"You think I'd involve my little girl in cleaning up this mess?" the man said. He pressed the gun's barrel to the base of Wayne's skull. "When I kill him, his brains will fly all over this room."

Wayne whimpered, and Daniel stiffened, searching for an angle to shut the bastard up.

"I've seen your work." He nodded at Daniel. He raised the gun, aiming it at Raven's chest. "Olivia, move away from him. Open the door to the wine cellar."

She looked around the room, her face panicked. She glanced back and forth between them.

Their captor let out a shout of laughter. "Holy hell. You don't remember anything, do you?" A gleam appeared in his eye. "Very interesting. I'll give you a clue. It's not the wooden door. Your ex thinks his wine collection is valuable enough to warrant protection. Maybe after this is over, I'll enjoy a few vintages."

The man chuckled, and Daniel gritted his teeth in frustration, letting out a vicious curse. The boot camp graduate kept perfect position. Daniel couldn't risk a frontal assault, not without casualties. He wouldn't be able to disarm the guy before Raven went down or her ex ate a bullet.

"If you don't want Wayne to die in front of you, I suggest you move, Olivia," their captor said.

Raven hurried across the floor. With a shaking hand, she flicked the latch. The metal door swung open with barely a wisp of sound.

"Please," she said, turning toward him. "I understand you love your daughter. We can work something out."

"You *bought* my daughter," he growled. "You stole her from us."

Raven shook her head. "No. I wouldn't have. I helped Chelsea—"

"Don't mention her name. I made her pay."

"You...you killed her?" Raven asked.

"She betrayed me." His eyes had gone crazy.

"You'll never get away with this," Daniel said, easing slowly toward their captor, working for an angle to attack.

He shook his head. "You have no idea what's going on

here, do you? You're all dead. No one's left who cares, no one to talk. We'll start over."

The guy's twitchy fingers flexed against the trigger. He was unpredictable, and that made him too dangerous.

"That's enough of your games. Olivia, come two steps toward me to give secret agent man plenty of room."

Raven moved, and Daniel cursed under his breath. A prime opportunity gone.

"Get inside that room," the man ordered Daniel.

With a deep breath, he walked through the steel door. The stone walls looked way too familiar. He paused at the entrance.

"I can shoot her right now," his captor said.

Daniel fought his own instincts not to make a mistake. He had backup. He just had to keep them both alive until Noah arrived with Elijah.

Raven met his gaze. Did she see the panic clawing up his insides?

She must have, because she nodded her head.

He took a few steps deeper into the room. Seconds later Raven stumbled inside, and the steel door slammed behind them.

With a worried expression, she gripped his hand. "Don't worry. I'll help you," she whispered. "I won't let you lose yourself."

Daniel blinked, eyeing another dungeon.

DUSK HAD FALLEN when Pamela pulled the stolen SUV in front of Wayne Harrison's house. Not a bad neighborhood...for now.

She leaned her head back against the leather seat. Her life as Pamela Winter ended here. Today. The terrified wife and mother were gone. A new woman had discovered strength enough to leave the past behind and begin again.

In a strange way, thanks to Olivia Harrison.

She picked up her cell phone and dialed her son's number.

"I have them," Christopher answered. "We've won, Mother. No one can take my girls away from me now. Not once I kill them all."

"Even her bodyguard?" Pamela asked.

Christopher lowered his voice. "Yeah. He's not so tough."

"Find out who else knows anything about our plans, then kill them. We'll save your daughters together. No one will ever steal them again." She studied the phone in her hand. This would be her last conversation with Christopher. She refused to regret it. He'd become just like his father.

Pamela glanced in the backseat. A box of dynamite sat in the floorboard. She'd hated her husband's business. She'd liked the money, but she'd hated being dirty and grimy. The only good thing about having to work with him in those early days was that she'd learned how to blow a hole in the ground.

She could blow a hole in this house.

The perfect plan. The perfect scapegoat.

"I'm going to enjoy this."

She recognized the eagerness in her son's voice. She remembered that same tone when he'd headed out for his hunting trips. She shivered. Her son was as certifiable as his father.

"We can't attract attention. I'm a half hour away, honey. Can you wait until dark? Better cover that way."

"I'll wait. You have the babies?"

"All packed up. We'll leave as soon as I get there." Pamela tossed the phone in the passenger's seat and picked up a throwaway cell she'd purchased at a drug store. She pocketed it and exited the vehicle.

A large dog stuck his nose out of a window of another SUV parked in front of Harrison's house. A deep bark escaped from him, then another.

Pamela froze. She looked around. No one seemed to be paying any attention. She stood still for several moments. Christopher didn't come to the door. They obviously couldn't hear the mutt inside the house.

She threw a rock at the car. The dog ducked down, then returned, still barking.

Damn it. She wouldn't have much time. Eventually the stupid canine would attract attention.

Ignoring the dog, she went to work. Within minutes she'd taken the box to the back of the house. Wayne Harrison had made it easy to stay hidden, with all the trees in his yard.

Within seconds she'd placed three of the four charges.

She stepped back and dialed 9-1-1.

"What's your emergency?" the voice asked.

A sob escaped Pamela's throat. "Please, please. Help. He's going to kill her. I know he is."

"Who are you talking about, ma'am?"

"My son. He's crazy. He just got out of the army. He wants to kill that woman I saw on the news. The woman without a memory. Her name is Olivia Harrison. He said he was going to kill her and her husband. I know he's going to their house. You have to stop him. He's taken my husband's gun and dynamite. He's going to kill them."

"Ma'am—"

With a smile, Pamela ended the call and tossed the phone on the last explosives. She bent down and set the final charge.

Soon her family would be safe. Her real family. Hope and Christina. Everything would be fine this time.

She was starting over.

THE STEEL DOOR slammed, and a lock turned. A small sliver of light filtered on the side of the darkening blinds from the single window near the ceiling.

Raven clutched Daniel's hands. Even in the dimness, his eyes were wild, with that same look she'd seen above the wash.

"Not a dungeon," he whispered. "A wine cellar. A wine cellar."

She cupped his face between her hands, desperate for him to see her, not those nightmarish visions. "You fought this battle once, Daniel. You can do it again. Look at me."

Daniel blinked, and the faraway look in his eyes cleared. He stared down at her, his hazel eyes holding her captive. He cupped her cheek. "Thank you. I'm back."

"I know," she said. "You always come back."

He didn't respond, and she prayed he believed her, but something told her Daniel would never be satisfied until the episodes never returned. She didn't know a lot about PTSD, but she couldn't imagine it was something that just stopped one day.

"We have to get out of here." Daniel grabbed the window jamb and lifted himself up, tearing down the covering. It didn't help much with the sun setting, but at least they could see the room more clearly. Several shelves lined the stone walls with bottle after bottle of wine. A few boxes were stacked in the corner, but there wasn't much else in the room.

"I think you can fit through this window, Raven. I got a signal off to Noah. He should be here soon, but I won't take a chance with your life."

"What about Hope?" she asked, gnawing on her lower lip. "He knows where she is. He has to."

"Once we're out of here and have backup, we'll get the information out of him. No matter what it takes." Daniel jumped down. "I need something to break the glass."

The wine bottles wouldn't cut it. Raven walked the edge of the room. They could break the shelves apart and hope the noise didn't attract attention. Or…

She grabbed a fire extinguisher from the corner. "Will this work?"

He grabbed her face and kissed her. "Brilliant." He held the extinguisher and looked around. "It'll make a lot of noise." He lifted a wine bottle and swung it down against the rack, shattering the end and leaving a jagged weapon behind.

They both held their breath, but the steel door didn't open.

"It'll be ten times worse when I break the window." He handed the broken bottle to Raven. "If that bastard opens the door don't hesitate. Do as much damage as you can."

Raven wouldn't have considered herself bloodthirsty, but after what that man had done, she didn't think she'd lose sleep if she had to carve up his face. Raven crouched near the door, clutching the neck of the jagged bottle with a death grip.

Daniel cleared the bottom two shelves and rigged a stool from the wooden parts. "This is it." He stepped up and heaved the extinguisher at the glass.

It shattered.

Using his jacket to protect his skin, Daniel shoved aside the remaining shards. "Okay, darlin'. Let's get you out of here. Noah should be here soon. Call the cops from a neighbor's house and hide until they get here."

She hesitated. "What about you?" Even she could

tell Daniel couldn't get his shoulders through the small window.

"I'll be fine."

Without another word, Daniel hefted Raven up. She stuck her head out of the window and let out a strangled gasp.

Wave upon wave of memories pummeled her. Unable to bear the agony, she let go and slid back into Daniel's arms, sagging against him.

"My God, you look like you're going to faint. What happened?"

Raven could barely catch her breath. "The woman outside," she panted. "I recognize her. Pamela Winter. She's the one who tried to kill me. She's the one who buried me alive." Raven gripped Daniel's shirt. "And I saw dynamite."

Chapter Twelve

Daniel hitched himself to see out the window. Sure enough, a woman in a designer suit held the ends of four wires and a detonator in her hands. He followed one of the wires to a bundle of dynamite. "She's going to blow the place," he hissed.

Suddenly, as if sensing their presence, she raised her head and searched her surroundings, her gaze narrow and suspicious.

"Lift me up," Raven ordered. "Maybe I can make her see sense."

They didn't have anything to lose.

"Pamela!" Raven yelled. "Don't do this. We can work it out."

"It's too late," Pamela bit out. "You wouldn't help me. You wanted to find out more damned information while my baby was dying. Now I'm claiming my family and yours."

"But—"

She slammed down the ancient dynamite blaster.

In a split second, Daniel grabbed Raven by the waist and threw them both behind one of the heavy wine racks, wedging themselves between the solid wood back and the stone wall. He sent up a small prayer for Raven and covered her with his body.

An explosion erupted, shaking the earth, then a second, third and fourth followed.

Dirt rained down, but the stone walls didn't crumble. The wine rack swayed and fell back, angled against the wall, but it held, making a small canopy over their hiding place.

Soon an odd quiet settled over them. Daniel pushed aside the wine rack and looked around. He peered outside the window. Black smoke poured from the house.

He stared around the small stone room. "The dungeon saved us," he muttered. The irony of it all. Christopher may have saved their lives by locking them away. But they weren't safe yet.

Daniel rushed to the steel door and placed his hand onto it. Heat burned his palm, and he snatched his hand away. "We have to get out of here."

He looked down. Smoke filtered in under the door.

"What about Wayne?" Raven asked.

Daniel pointed to the foggy tendrils. "The fire's already here. We can't open the door. If Wayne survived, they're already out."

Her eyes widened. She gave a sharp nod. She knew. Both men were probably dead.

Daniel bent down below the window and folded his hands together. "Come on. Climb through that window."

He heaved her up, and she squeezed her torso through the window. The smoke formed a wall behind Daniel, like a death call. He coughed. They were out of time.

"Hurry," he said as the smoke rose, pushing her hips through the small opening. Suddenly Raven slipped from his hands.

"Daniel, are you in there?"

At Noah's shout, Daniel sent up a prayer of thanks. He hefted himself up. "Get her out of here," he said, coughing.

"She's fine," Noah said. Daniel's shoulders struck against the window jamb. He sucked in a breath of air. "Get a crowbar."

Noah took off. Smoke billowed into the room on either side of him. He blinked back the stinging from his eyes.

"Hold your breath and move out of the way," Noah said. "I'll be as fast as I can. I only need a few inches."

Daniel released his hold and fell back into the wine cellar. The smoke had gotten so thick he couldn't see anything. He kept one hand on the jamb. If he let go, he could die in here.

"Back away, Daniel! We have a sledgehammer."

Keeping his hand against the stone wall, Daniel eased away. His lungs burned. He couldn't hold his breath much longer.

The wall shook. Two strikes later, stone crumbled over him. "That's it!" Noah yelled. "Get out here!" he shouted through a series of coughs.

Spots in front of his eyes, Daniel followed his touch to the opening. His hands curved over the window's edge and two hands grabbed him, dragging him out of the burning building.

Noah didn't stop until he'd dragged Daniel ten feet away, then he fell back onto his butt.

Daniel sucked in a lungful of air, and a coughing fit hit.

"Damn, you almost ended up as barbecue," Noah said. "How did you avoid that?"

Blinking the smoke out of his eyes, Daniel stared at the inferno Wayne Harrison's house had become. Fire spewed into the sky; black smoke billowed upward. "Stone wine cellar. Strongest room in the house," he said, still coughing as his gaze swept through the rescue personnel, looking for one dark-haired woman. "Where's Raven?"

"Paramedics have her."

Daniel stumbled to his feet. “Is she going to be all right?”

He scanned the chaotic scene and headed to the emergency vehicles. His heart raced, and then he saw her, face smudged, an oxygen mask on, Trouble at her feet—but she was safe.

Daniel’s knees buckled in relief, and Noah grabbed his arm.

A fireman ran up to them. “Anyone left in there?”

Noah nodded. “Two. In the basement adjacent to the room where you found us. The door was hot.”

The man nodded and ran toward his teammates, and Daniel lurched toward Raven. He knelt in front of her. “You’re okay?”

“You saved me. Again.”

Daniel hugged close the woman who’d once more almost died because of him. “Thank God you’re all right.”

“Do you know who did this?” Noah asked.

“Her name is Pamela Winter,” Raven said. She met Daniel’s gaze, her eyelashes wet with tears. “I remember. The moment I saw Pamela, I remembered everything.”

PAMELA RUBBED HER face with her hands. She should have used a timer. Stupid mistake. The explosion had sent debris flying, shattering her windshield. She’d wasted precious minutes taking back streets so she wouldn’t get stopped by the cops.

Finally she’d reached the exchange point, dumping the stolen SUV for the car Hector had set up. The car she’d take north to her new life.

Pamela didn’t bother parking in long-term. She had to get her daughters and leave.

Now that everyone who could steal her life was dead, everything would be okay. Christina would get well. She and her daughters would live the good life. Away from Trouble, Texas.

She tapped her foot waiting for the elevator. Finally the metal doors slid open. She pressed the number for the pediatric floor. This would be the hardest part, getting the girls out without anyone seeing.

She might have to put them in a laundry cart. She'd attract attention with two babies in her arms.

The doors slid open, and she walked past the nurses' station.

"Mrs. Winter?" A solemn-faced nurse flagged her down. "I need you to come with me."

Pamela's throat closed. They couldn't possibly know anything. Olivia and Wayne Harrison were dead. Christopher was dead. She was home free. She struggled to tamp down the panic.

"After I make sure my daughters are all right." Pamela quickened her pace down the hall.

The nurse followed. "That's what I need to talk to you about."

When Pamela reached the small room with two cribs, she skidded to a halt. One was empty.

"Where's Christina?" Pamela whirled around at the nurse, wanting to strike out. *"Where's my daughter?"*

The nurse stepped back warily. "She's in the Pediatric Intensive Care Unit. She developed a heart arrhythmia. They're doing everything they can to stabilize her."

THE FIRE HOSES sent several arcs of water onto the burning house, and the sky filled with hissing steam. Despite the firefighters' efforts, the conflagration continued to crackle and burn. Smoke stung Raven's eyes. She still couldn't believe Pamela Winter had done this.

Daniel stood at the edge of the emergency vehicles talking urgently to one of the cops. They shook hands, and Daniel strode over to her. "They've put out an APB on Pamela, but I had to tell him I didn't know the identity of the man who locked us in the wine cellar. They'll want to talk to you."

She tapped her temple. "I've seen him before…or I've seen his picture, but where?" She grabbed her head. "Why won't my memory work?"

Daniel squatted down in front of her. "It'll come to you, but for now, do you have any idea where Pamela went?"

Raven bit her lip. "Try the hospitals. Search for Christina Winter."

"Who is that?"

"Chelsea's daughter." Raven rose and paced back and forth. "Pamela called me and told me that Chelsea had given birth to twins. I never knew, Daniel. If there had been two, I would have taken both of them. She told me that her daughter was ill and that Hope might be able to help. I agreed to a blood test so they could determine if the girls matched. They more than matched. They're identical."

Two firefighters let out a shout and raced away from Wayne's house. A wall fell, and the flames licked at least twenty feet in the air. The lot had turned to hell.

"Pamela invited me to her house to meet her daughter. I brought Hope." She shook her head. "If only I hadn't taken her with me."

"You couldn't have known," Daniel interrupted.

"When I got there, Pamela started talking about surgery and anesthesia. I wanted to help, but I couldn't sign a consent form without getting an opinion. Hope was only eighteen months old. I needed to understand the risks."

Raven clutched the locket. "She went crazy, starting screaming and yelling about how I was killing her daughter. I got upset and tried to leave, but she screamed, 'No!'

Then she shoved me." Raven pressed her hand to her forehead. "That's the last thing I remember until I awoke trapped in the mine. I'm so lucky you found me."

Daniel motioned to the cop and gave him Christina's name. Raven's eyes widened. "I just remembered where I saw the guy from the basement. His picture was on Pamela's wall."

"Really?" Daniel tugged out his phone and tapped in a few lines. Within seconds he turned the phone around, showing her a graduation photo. "Christopher Winter. He was Pamela's son."

"She killed her own son? Oh, God, she really is crazy. And she has Hope. And Christina."

Noah raced over to them, his expression grim.

Raven bit her lip. "What's wrong?"

"They found Hope," Noah said. "She's in the hospital." He frowned. "Unfortunately Christina is in intensive care."

Daniel grasped Raven's elbow and guided her toward the SUV. "Then that's where we're going. Tell the cops. I hope they intercept Pamela before she gets to the twins."

"CHRISTINA CAN'T BE in ICU," Pamela insisted, her desperation mounting. "She was doing fine earlier."

"I'm sorry." The nurse gave Pamela's back a comforting pat, and Pamela fought to keep herself from shoving the stupid woman away.

"The doctor wants to make sure she's stable enough for the procedure tomorrow. She was definitely struggling for a while. He wants her in ICU so she'll have constant monitoring and extra care to prepare for the bone marrow transplant. It's not her first arrhythmia, but this bout took a lot out of her."

Pamela rubbed her arms to ward off the chill of the nurse's words. "But Christina is stable now?"

"Yes. For the past hour. I just checked on her progress."

Pamela clenched her fists. Damn it, she'd been *so* close to getting the babies away. She paused. If Christina wasn't in immediate danger, then maybe the plan would still work. *If* Pamela could get her daughter out of the ICU. Of course, the unit had ridiculously tight controls and constant monitoring, but Pamela had a gun.

No contest on who would win that one.

"Can I see her?"

The nurse smiled. "I'll take you."

Pamela glanced over at Hope, the girl's bone marrow the cure for her deathly ill daughter. Taking the eighteen-month-old into ICU wasn't an option. Pamela would have to come back for Hope.

Pamela followed the nurse down the hall. She buzzed into ICU, and they stepped inside.

"I'd like to see Christina Winter."

"You'll have to put on scrubs and a mask first."

After dressing, Pamela walked to the sixth crib. They'd attached Christina to a heart monitor and an IV. "Can I be alone with her?"

"You have five minutes. That's it until next hour."

After the nurse left, Pamela glanced down at her gown. She'd grabbed the largest one possible. Was it big enough to hide a too-small baby? It had to be.

Pamela leaned down to Christina. "Mommy's going to get you out of here."

Her daughter's eyes blinked, and she smiled at her mother, a weak smile, but the baby reached out her hand and gripped Pamela's finger.

Her adrenaline was racing. "Mommy can do this, baby girl." Pamela had to time everything perfectly. If they turned their backs, she could rush out.

Her own heart pounding, she twisted one of the EKG

wires until it snapped. A monitor screeched, and Pamela threw open the curtain. "Something's wrong. Please, help her."

The nurse rushed into the room and silenced the machine.

"She was thrashing a bit, and then the monitor went off," Pamela said.

"One of the wires is damaged. I'll find another set and be right back." The nurse smiled. "She should be okay. It will only take a few minutes to hook her up."

"Thank you," Pamela said.

The nurse closed the curtain behind her.

Pamela unhooked the IV. Christina cried a bit, but Pamela tucked the baby against her chest, wrapping her in a blanket. Most people wouldn't stop someone in hospital clothes if they were in a hurry. She thought she heard the sound of sirens in the distance and panicked for a minute, then realized it was probably an ambulance heading for the E.R.

She held the baby close and grabbed the fabric curtain, wondering if the nurse had returned yet.

Suddenly a speaker squawked above her. "Code Black. This is not a drill. Code Black."

A vise clamped around her chest. What did that mean? Was someone dying?

She peeked around the curtain.

Two policemen entered ICU, and the nurse pointed at Pamela.

No. This couldn't be happening.

Pamela lunged through the curtain, clasping the baby to her. She bolted for the elevator.

One of the cops veered to the left to head her off. "Ma'am. You have to stop."

The nurse picked up the phone. "Security. Pamela Winter is in PICU. She has taken her daughter."

"Leave me alone!" Pamela screamed. "She's *my* daughter. I have the right to take her out of here."

The policeman stepped closer. "Just hand me the baby. Everything will be fine."

Pamela shook her head. "Nothing is fine. Everything is wrong. We're supposed to be gone."

"You're not leaving here with that baby."

The other cop snapped, "She's not going anywhere but a jail cell."

Pamela's entire body stilled. *They knew.* Somehow they knew what she'd done. They would take Christina away from her.

"No. No one can take care of Christina but me."

She whipped her husband's gun from her pocket. "Stay back!" She aimed the weapon at the nurse, and the cops froze. "My daughter and I are leaving. Try to stop me, even make a move toward your weapons, and you're dead."

Pamela backed up until she reached the ICU door's entrance, pushed through, then raced down the hall. She skidded to a halt when two security guards rounded the corner.

"Stop!"

The baby started screaming. *Oh, God, don't let her have a heart attack.* Frantic, Pamela whirled around and bolted toward the door to the stairs. She shoved through, and the metal door slammed off the wall.

Thundering footsteps pounded toward her from behind and from below.

A security guard yelled, "You can't escape now! You're trapped."

"No! Get away from me! She's mine!" Tears blurred her vision, but she fired two shots down into the stairwell.

The men ducked momentarily, but then started coming after her again.

Hysteria had her feeling like her mind was going to explode.

"Leave me alone! You're scaring her."

She fired off two more bullets, and heard the pained cry of one of her pursuers.

Clutching the terrified baby tighter, Pamela turned and ran higher, tripping over the stairs in her fatigue. There was only one floor left. Would the door be open?

If not, could she reach the roof?

Maybe she could bolt the door? Or there might be a fire escape? Didn't all buildings have to have one?

A man grabbed her ankle, and she whirled and shot him point blank in the head. He fell back and tumbled down the stairs, dead. One more obstacle behind her.

"Don't follow me. I will kill you all," she yelled into the emptiness.

She stumbled her way onto the top floor landing, ragged breaths sawing in and out of her chest, and yanked on the door but it was locked. "No!"

Sobbing now, she headed to the next door, marked Exit, probably to the roof, so she burst through and slammed the door, then shot at it until there were no bullets left in the gun. She jammed the door with her revolver.

Her mind inundated by crazy thoughts, she couldn't think, she could only clutch Christina tight. Pamela staggered out onto the wide expanse. Far below, sirens and lights flashed. Dozens of police cars and fire engines surrounded the hospital. A SWAT team vehicle pulled up, and soon snipers poured out of the back.

Oh, God, they were going to kill her.

She sank to her knees, rocking the baby to and fro. "All I wanted was for you and me to be happy. I won't give you up, baby girl. I can't."

FIFTEEN MINUTES COULD be an eternity. Daniel swerved into the hospital parking lot and the SUV screeched to a halt, Noah and Elijah on his tail. He grabbed Raven's hand, and they raced to the entrance.

Two cops blocked them. "I'm sorry, sir. The hospital is on lockdown."

"Frank Detry, the SWAT negotiator, requested us," Daniel said, his voice firm. They didn't have time for this. "We have information about Pamela Winter."

Expression skeptical, the cop muttered a few words into his radio. His eyes widened. "Follow me."

The cop led them to the elevator, and he punched the top floor button. They exited, and a solemn-looking man with a military haircut walked over to them. "I'm Detry. Thank you for coming." His gaze pinned Raven. "Pamela Winter wants to see you. She's threatened to jump off the roof with her baby if she can't talk to you."

Raven blanched. "What about the little girl called Hope Harrison? Maybe she's been listed as Hope Winter? She's my daughter."

"She's fine. She's on the pediatric floor, in no danger. I'd like to tell you that you can see her now, but I need your help. I don't know how much longer my team can keep Pamela talking."

Daniel cut him off. "No way in hell are you going up there, Raven. This woman's already tried to kill you twice. Hell, she blew up her own son."

"I have to go," Raven insisted. "That poor frightened baby never did anything to anyone. Her mother is dead. So is her father. She's Hope's sister. Her twin. Who's going to look out for Christina if not me?"

Daniel couldn't fight her. He'd have done the same thing. But he also knew she wouldn't be out there alone. No way. No how. "I'm going with you."

"I checked you and CTC out," Detry said. "We could use you. Come with me."

In the stairwell leading to the roof, the SWAT team fit Raven with a bulletproof vest. "She has a gun, and she shot a few security guards and killed a cop, but she hasn't fired it in the past half hour. We're hoping she's out of ammo, but we don't know that for certain. The door is barricaded. If you can get her away from the roof's edge, we can take her out."

"You can't attack. She's holding a baby."

"We'll try to stop her other ways, but if she starts shooting again, all bets are off."

Daniel walked Raven to the door and turned her in his arms. "You really want to do this?"

"No. I'm petrified, but I'm the only chance that child has."

"You'll stay safe. No crazy chances. Promise?" He touched her cheek. "Come back to me?"

"Now?" she said incredulously. "Now you get mushy on me?"

"Come back to me, and I'll work on my timing."

She went up on tiptoe and kissed him on the lips. "I'll be back. You've given me another incentive."

The SWAT negotiator hammered on the door to the roof. "Mrs. Winter, we've met your demands. Olivia is here."

They heard scraping at the door, then it swung part of the way open.

"Send her out alone, or Christina dies." Pamela's voice became more distant with every word.

When Raven looked around the door, she saw Pamela had returned to her spot on the ledge. The baby looked very ill. Her weak cries broke Raven's heart.

"Pamela?" Raven called. "Your baby is sick and needs care. Please let me help you."

The woman whirled. "Help me? My baby is *dying,* and it's all your fault. You wanted to wait. Get another opinion before the transplant. Christina didn't have time to wait. *You did this to her!*"

Fear struck Raven's heart. "Please, Pamela, come away from the edge. We can work this out."

"Sure. You'd like that," Pamela raved. "You know they're going to take Christina away from me. I bet you wanted them both all the time."

A grappling hook flew over the edge of the roof. She stiffened, desperate not to give anything away. *Daniel?* She had to make certain Pamela didn't look his way. She shifted positions. "I was happy with Hope. I wanted to help you. *I intended to help you.*"

Pamela paced on the ledge, her movements erratic.

"But you had to wait. Then you had to hit your head. I only pushed you a little. You tripped on a toy. You messed up everything."

DANIEL HELD ON to the rope, slowly inching his way up from the top floor window to the roof. Elijah and Noah were climbing up the opposite side. Hopefully Winter didn't have three bullets left, or the surprise would be theirs instead. Daniel hauled himself quietly over the roof ledge, ignoring the agony in the hand and leg that had been shattered in Bellevaux.

An air-conditioning duct blocked him from Winter's view, and a lot of space separated him from the two women. Pamela looked at Raven with such hatred that a chill invaded Daniel.

"Get on the ledge with me." Pamela aimed the gun at Raven's head. "Now."

She'd *promised* him she'd stay safe. When they made it off this roof, he'd...he'd kiss her until he forgot this moment ever happened. Daniel's heart stuck in his throat as Raven stepped onto the narrow lip of the building.

Wind buffeted both women, but Raven had the added disadvantage of the recent concussion, and she wobbled precariously on the thin concrete shelf.

"Please," Raven begged, holding out her arms. "Let me take the baby inside."

Pamela waved the gun at Raven.

"She's mine. No one else can have her," Pamela raged. "If you'd just done what you were told, Christina would have gotten her treatment already. She'd be cured."

Raven took a step forward. "The doctors can still help her, Pamela. Don't give up on your daughter."

Daniel caught Noah's profile in the corner of his eye and spotted two SWAT snipers on the roof across the way. If Pamela would only give Raven the baby.

Raven was way too close to her, though. If Pamela went over, she could take Raven down with her.

"Christopher is dead. I killed my own son. You really think they're ever going to let me see her again? What do I have left?"

"Christina isn't going to die if you let her go back inside the hospital now," Raven argued. She took one step closer, and Pamela turned to face her, her back toward Daniel.

He leaned forward then ran silently ahead. He couldn't cry out a warning, not without making things worse. His fists clenched, he crouched in position, waiting for an opportunity.

Pamela peered over the side, and a cry went up from the crowd. "They want me to jump, those animals." Christina whimpered, and Pamela hugged the baby closer. "That's the kind of world I'd be leaving her in. She's better off dead. We both are.

"Ashes, ashes, we all fall down..."

Pamela bent over, staring at the street below. "It's time to end this."

Raven reached toward Pamela. "Don't. Please."

"I'm not going alone. You're coming with me." Pamela grabbed Raven's arm and headed over the side.

Daniel lunged for Raven, arms outstretched. He barely grasped her wrist before she fell. His entire body tensed, and he yanked her to safety.

Elijah and Noah came in from the other side and snagged hold of Pamela, but she was already dangling off the roof, fighting them violently. "Let me go!"

Daniel raced back to the edge. The crowd below shouted and pointed. The firemen had a large trampoline set up to catch anyone who fell, but Daniel knew the baby would never survive a fall from that height by herself.

Pamela jerked against Elijah and Noah, and the baby slipped from her arms.

Pamela had lost her hold on the baby.

Daniel dove off the roof and grabbed the baby as she fell. The ground came up fast, and just before he landed, he twisted, landing on his back on the trampoline, Christina cradled in his arms.

Pamela screamed, berserk now, biting Elijah's hand and breaking his hold. Noah still had her, but he was dragged halfway over the ledge, scrambling for a foothold and struggling to keep his grip on her. Elijah lay on his belly, grabbing for her again, but she slammed her gun hard against Noah's head and pushed away from him.

She aimed at Raven, who had come up behind Noah to help.

"I saved one for you," Pamela said and pulled the trigger just as Noah shoved her aside.

Daniel watched from down below, frozen, as Pamela whirled around, lost her balance and plummeted to the ground. The firemen who were helping Daniel and the baby from the trampoline had no time to move it to save her.

Daniel clutched the baby protectively to his chest, shielding her from the sight. His heart filled with the most incredible tenderness as the tiny little one sobbed weakly and curled in closer to him.

Raven exited the hospital and ran into Daniel's arms. "Is it over?"

"It's over, and this precious girl needs a doctor."

Raven looked at the possessive way he was holding Christina and smiled. "It looks like she's already worked some of her own medicine."

Daniel felt the cold, dark places inside him start to fill with a healing warmth as he thought of the future. "You may be right."

THE EIGHT DAYS that had passed after the events on the roof could have easily been eighty. Dressed in an isolation suit, Raven rocked Christina, her slight weight barely registering. The chemo had taken its toll, but Christina was holding her own. The little girl let out a small yawn, then settled in for a nap. Her pale face remained wan, and every night Raven hit her knees in prayer that the transplant would work. She'd fallen in love with Hope's twin, who looked so much like her daughter. And yet they were very different. Hope had a light about her. Christina was an old soul. Quiet, a follower, but always watching.

At first the hospital wouldn't let Raven see Christina, but Daniel had come to their rescue once again. When social services had sent in a caseworker, he'd called CTC. She didn't know who Ransom Grainger was, besides head of CTC, but the man had major connections. He'd provided her with an attorney, and now Raven had temporary custody of Christina, hoping to make it permanent. The lawyer thought they had a good chance because of Hope.

Raven prayed he was right.

She pushed the rocker back and forth until Christina's breathing became slow and regular, then she placed her in her ICU crib. With a last look at the little girl who had been through so much, she quietly exited the isolation ward.

Outside, she removed the protective clothing and mask and leaned back against the door. Her eyes burned with unshed tears. What if Christina didn't make it? She didn't want to lose her now.

She felt an arm pull her close. She didn't have to open her eyes to know his touch, his scent. She leaned into Daniel.

"How is she?" he whispered.

"She's so weak, so tired. I'm scared."

"She's a fighter, too. I've seen those determined eyes."

Raven smiled. "She is that. Where's Hope?"

"Your daughter is now trying to keep up with Ethan, the son of my sheriff buddy, Blake, and his wife, Amanda, from Carder. They took her for pizza. Ethan has decided he's going to marry her someday."

"Let's get her out of diapers first," Raven said. She rested her head against Daniel's chest. "I hope I did the right thing in okaying the transplant."

"If it had been Hope—"

"I would have done the same thing." She gave him a tired smile. "Thank you."

"For what?"

"For being here. Most wouldn't want to be bothered."

Daniel rubbed the nape of his neck. "You needed me. I told you that I'd be here as long as you needed me." He held out his hand. "How about some fresh air?"

She nodded, and they left the hospital. Trouble trotted right beside Daniel, following them into an open area before settling in the grass and watching them.

Ignoring their canine voyeur, she breathed in and stared at the man beside her. She wanted to ask him a question, but she was afraid of the answer. However, her heart needed to know. "How long are you staying?"

He dropped her hand and stepped back. "Do you want me to leave?"

"I never want you to leave." Raven couldn't meet his gaze. "If you'd asked me a few weeks ago if I would or could fall in love in a few days, I would have called you crazy. Daniel, I fell in love with you."

He stared at her, open-mouthed.

Heat rose in her cheeks. "Yeah, that's what I thought you'd say. I need someone in my life who wants a family. I have two girls to look after. I can't—" Her voice broke. "If you don't want the same, I…I can't be around you anymore. It makes me want…more than you can give."

"What do you want?" His eyes burned into her, holding her captive.

"I've seen you with Hope. You're always here, always caring. You make my heart race when you touch me. I love you, Daniel Adams, but I don't think you feel the same."

"You're wrong." He pressed his lips softly to hers. Raven's entire body collapsed against him. "I love you, Raven. You gave me stillness and peace that I never thought I'd find. You touched me in that wine cellar and drove away my demons. But more than that, I've watched you with Christina. I've watched you love that little girl you didn't know. You gave her the strength to fight. How could I not love you?"

With a shudder, Daniel held her close.

She shivered against him, and Daniel closed his eyes. "I want to be there for you. Forever. Always. I want to love you, the girls and any children we may want in the future. But it's a risk, honey. Those demons will always be there for me. All I can promise is that I'll fight them for you, for the children."

She leaned away and cupped Daniel's cheek. "If you'll fight, I'll be there by your side, Daniel. I will never give up on you. I'll never give up on Christina or Hope."

"Then I have just one question, my love." Daniel knelt on the grass. Raven stared down at him; her breath caught. He pulled a box from his pocket. A bullet casing tumbled out with it, landing on the grass.

Daniel stared at the bit of brass, but didn't pick it up. Instead he held out her ring. "Will you marry me? Can you love me, despite my flaws and my fears?"

She knelt next to him. "I will marry you, Daniel."

He slipped the diamond on her hand. "I promise you, Raven, to never give up. On life, on love, or on you."

Epilogue

Darkness surrounded Daniel. Above him, below him, around him, he could feel the walls against his shoulders.

The nylon play tunnel rippled along him. A joyful giggle tinkled through the darkness, then another joined in the chorus. Finally two small figures collapsed onto his chest and hugged him.

"You captured me, my little princesses." He laughed softly. "What am I going to do?"

A light flicked on, and Daniel looked behind him through one of the open ends of the tunnel. Raven stood in the doorway with her hands on her hips, Trouble sitting at her feet. "You're all going to wash your hands for dinner, that's what you're going to do. Daddy has to study for his big exam."

His two girls ran to their mother and wrapped their arms around her legs. She knelt down and kissed each nose. "I'll be checking those hands, ladies."

"Okay, Mommy!"

Hope grabbed her sister's hand and dragged her off to the bathroom. Hope was such a little mother to her twin, probably because Chrissy had been so sick for so long.

Trouble wagged his tail and followed the girls.

At four years of age, they'd grown so much since those dark days.

"Chrissy's color is good." Daniel crossed the room to his wife.

His wife.

His heart flooded with satisfaction. He'd never thought he would be here. Never imagined, after everything that had happened with his father and Daniel's captivity, that he would find any kind of peace. Now he was over a year into getting a doctorate in psychology to specialize in helping victims of PTSD.

Not only had Raven quieted his soul, she'd filled his heart.

She burrowed her face into Daniel's chest and wrapped her arms around his waist, leaning into him. "The doctor was supposed to call today. He hasn't called. That can't be good."

"We'll deal with whatever comes our way." Daniel lowered his mouth to hers, tasting her lips with a promise. "Never give up. On life, on love, on each other. Wasn't that our vow?"

"Always." Her eyes held a tinge of fear. Neither one of them had allowed themselves to think beyond the bone marrow transplant. They couldn't. He wrapped his arm around Raven, and together they walked down the stairs.

The girls stood on the landing, wet hands outstretched, identical grins on their faces. Just as Raven bent over to inspect the job, the phone rang.

She froze. Daniel plucked the receiver from the base unit. "Hello?"

He strode over to her and leaned her back against him, tilting the phone so she could hear. His body tensed, bracing himself for the worse.

"We received Christina's tests results, Mr. Adams. Her blood work is as normal as it can be."

Raven's knees gave way, and Daniel took her full weight. He couldn't stop grinning.

"We'll run the test periodically," the doctor added, "but I think we're out of the woods. Congratulations."

Their daughters, sensing something had happened, stopped their playing. Chrissy looked up at her parents. "What's wrong, Mommy?"

Hope gripped her sister's hand. "Is Chrissy sick again, Mama?" The girl's eyes grew wet with unshed tears.

Daniel raced across the room and grabbed one daughter in each arm. "Everybody's well." He whirled them around. "We're having a celebration. Ice cream all around."

"Yea!" The twins escaped his embrace, skidded to the kitchen and stared intently up at the freezer.

Daniel held out his hand, and Raven linked her fingers with his. He kissed the tips one by one, and she shivered.

"How about a date tonight? We could make some more memories," Daniel said, his voice low and full of promise.

Raven's eyes flared with passion, and Daniel smiled at the love shining just for him.

She leaned into him, her weight trusting and true. "Memories we'll never forget."

* * * * *